MINE to Protect

Sarah J. Brooks

ISBN-13: 978-1987691962

ISBN-10: 1987691962

Author's note: This is a work of fiction. Some of the names and geographical locations in this book are products of the author's imagination, and do not necessarily correspond with reality.

Mine to Protect

For my readers

Table of contents

Prologue

Paul

I'd been planning my moves for the entire year and the object of my obsession was running across the lawn with the gazelle legs I'd dreamed about.

"I can't believe we're almost out of here!" Gwen's voice rang out across the lawn at Dover High School. She was about to graduate. I'd graduated the year before, but she never noticed me. She and her friends were "the herd" all the other girls wanted to be a part of, and all the guys wanted to date. Gwen, with her sexy coloring of milky blonde hair and deep turquoise eyes was, by default, the girl all the wannabes copied. Who wouldn't? She was tall, with breasts that spilled out of her clothes, endless legs topped by slim hips and an even slimmer waist. She looked like a high-priced model. Everyone said so and at some point, I think Gwen began to believe it herself. It wasn't vanity. Nobody knew she was shy. I knew, though...I'd been watching her for two years. I knew she passed her eighteenth birthday two weeks earlier. Now I had my chance.

The girls copied everything she did. I got a kick out of it. She'd wear deep purple one day and the next, it was all over the school. The other boys could only stare and imagine what she looked like without her clothes. They'd never get to see her up close.

Cheerleading was over for her senior year and she was on her way to the gym, carrying her pompoms. I cruised by the school at three-thirty, just in time to watch her. The lawn beside the school was her personal practice field. I'd parked a half block away and watched as she bent that body into somersaults and splits, her pale hair catching the breeze like a mainsail on an early spring day. I got hard just watching her; imagining those splits opened over my lap. Students waiting for their bus stood so they could watch, too, but I didn't like to think about any of them getting hard over my girl. That's how I thought of her—as my girl. I bragged when she took first place in the state with her cheerleading routine. She'd probably made one helluva gymnast if she'd been shorter. Tall girls became models, not gymnasts. Too bad. I'd always wanted to fuck a gymnast, but I'd never trade Gwen for one. Not on your life.

Talk was, that occasionally one of the boys would dare ask her out on a date. Gwen was friendly, but word got around quickly that she was a virgin and not planning to change. The boys found it just too miserable to be with her; to touch her, to see her smile close and find those turquoise eyes staring up at them—but not be able to touch her. Not *really* touch her.

I was pretty sure she didn't have a clue who I was, even though I hadn't been a slouch when it came to the popularity rankings myself. I'd had my share and turned down even more. She was different. I wanted her. I would have her.

Gwen

We were lined up alphabetically which meant I was more than three-quarters away from the front, but that was fine. I liked sitting toward the back where I could see so many of my classmates. I knew this might be the last time I'd ever see some of them. The idea made me sad, but it also meant I was off to a new beginning—one I couldn't wait to start.

As my eyes drifted over the graduates and into the bleachers, I couldn't help but notice someone staring straight at me. He was sitting almost directly next to my row, so I could see him well. At first, I was embarrassed to have caught him staring and looked away. I looked back three more times from the corner of my eye and his eyes were still fixated on me.

"Patsy, is there something wrong with me?" I whispered to the girl to my right.

"Wrong?"

"There's a guy over there, staring at me. Is something torn, unzipped or about to fall off me?"

She looked me over and frowned. "Not that I can see."

I was uncomfortable. "Look over my shoulder, into

the bleachers, about the third row up. Do you see a guy staring at me?"

She slowly swiveled her head, so she wouldn't be obvious and looked straight ahead again before nodding. "Yes."

"What's the matter with him?"

She shrugged and rolled her eyes. "Wish he was staring at me. That's Paul Romano. He graduated last year. He is *so* hot. Girls threw themselves at him; in fact, I heard one girl swallowed a bottle of aspirin to get his attention."

I stared at her, my mouth opened. "Was she okay?"

Patsy shrugged again. "I guess so. It was almost the end of the year; senior prom and I think she thought he was going to ask her and then didn't. I didn't hear she died, and I almost always hear who dies because my older sister does the hair of the dead people at Trinkle's Funeral Home."

I shuddered and felt sorry for the girl. I couldn't imagine ever trying to take my life over a guy. Then I felt a little sorry for myself. I'd never been in love with anyone enough to do something like that. I wondered what that kind of adoration would feel like.

"Here we go," Patsy said as she elbowed me. It was time for our row to stand and file into the center aisle. I saw my parents sitting in the stands near the front and smiled. Mom waved frantically, and Dad nodded in that understated, authoritative way that bankers all behaved.

Principal Darren handed me my diploma and shook my hand. He passed me on to the superintendent whose name I couldn't remember and then I was following Patsy off the podium and alongside the seating to our row. I sneaked a quick peek and that Paul guy was grinning broadly, flashing me a thumbs-up. *What was the matter with him? I didn't even know him.*

Then it was over, we tossed our caps into the air and hugged one another. I knew Mom and Dad had a huge party planned with all the relatives willing to make the drive, so I posed for pictures and then hurried off to my locker for the last time. I twisted the combination and reached for my purse when a shadow loomed next to me.

"You did a great job," said a man's voice and it startled me. I looked up to see Paul Romano, a white grin on a tanned face that included a square jaw and sparkling brown eyes. I had to admit he was nice-looking.

"Do I know you?" I asked pensively.

"You will. Paul Romano is the name. I've just been waiting for you to graduate."

"Why?"

"Because you're going to dinner with me this Saturday and I don't date kids still in school."

"I think you forgot something," I shot back at him.

"What's that?"

"I haven't been asked and haven't agreed to go. I'm not sure I like the way you're acting, to tell you the truth."

"How am I acting?"

"You're going way too fast. Look, I need to get going. My parents are waiting. There's a party at the house."

"Good."

I looked at him, questioning.

"I'm your date."

"No, you're not. I don't know you and this is my party. Now, if you'll excuse me..."

"I'll walk you out."

There were people around and it seemed faster to just ignore him than stand and argue. Families of my friends were grabbing me along the way, hugging me and some pressed an envelope into my hand. I hadn't counted on that, but it was welcomed because I had a trip planned and every cent would come in handy.

I finally got as far as my car. Mom and Dad pulled up next to me and Mom's window rolled down. "We'll see you at home," she said. "Have we met your friend?" she asked. Mom was always very socially polite.

"He's not... no, you haven't. Mom, Dad, this is Paul Romano; Paul, my parents."

"Nice to meet you, Paul," Mom said politely. "Have Gwennie bring you to the party," she added as her window went up and Dad impatiently tapped his horn at a crowd that had gathered in front of their car.

"Well, well," Paul said to me, that disarming grin having an effect. "Looks like I'm invited after all."

"Look, I don't know what you want from me, but this is a special night and I really don't know you. It's an open house, so you can come if you want, but you'll have to drive yourself and I'll be tied up with all the guests. 711 Orchard Street, gray house on the corner." I got into my car.

"I know," he said as he closed my door, in a way that sort of spooked me but I decided to ignore him and get home. I looked in my rearview for the briefest of seconds to see him headed toward a truck. I wasn't sure how to feel about him, but it didn't matter, because I was leaving Brookfield behind as soon as I got enough money for my fare and a couple months' living expenses in Chicago. I had it in my head to become a model and I sure couldn't get there from Brookfield.

Paul pulled into my drive right behind me and before I could get out he was there, offering his arm and helping me carry the dress bag with my commencement robe and shoes. "Ah, thanks," I said awkwardly as we walked up to the house. I couldn't say he was exactly stalking me, but there was something a little odd about him. I felt like I was...well...prey.

My mother met me as I emerged from the house into the yard. "I'm glad you're here, we were starting to worry."

"Where did all these people come from?"

"They're your guests, dear."

"But, so many. It makes me feel like some kind of movie star."

"Well, stay grounded and keep an eye on those envelopes. There's money in them," she said, pointing to my handful with what was her normal level of worried suspicion. There were more money envelopes and as the night went on, I could feel Chicago coming closer and closer. Mom had ordered a champagne fountain and even though I wasn't legally allowed to drink yet, it was my party and Dad gave me the permission nod.

"Woah!" I moaned, dizzy. It went straight to my head. It felt like my heels were corkscrews and I couldn't seem to put one foot in front of the other. Paul was continually at my side, letting me lean against him when the room spun and holding his arm at the back of my waist to steady me. I kept drinking and every time I looked at him, he got better looking and I minded a little less that he was glued to my side.

The music started, and the lights went momentarily black before the colored disco ball Mom had insisted on lit up and shattered beams of light over everyone on the temporary dance floor. I thought I was doing well, but people seemed to keep running into me. Paul kept me supplied with champagne and when a slow song came up, he pulled me against him, hard. I could feel his privates were rigid and probing into me. For some reason, it didn't bother me one bit.

I knew it was late because there were fewer and fewer dancers and the dew was heavy on Dad's carefully manicured lawn. The caterers were beginning to package the remaining food into covered tins and finally, the fountain was disassembled and then it was completely gone. Mom and Dad had gone inside, and I could hear Mom giggling through their partially opened bedroom window. I tried not to listen, not to mentally picture them and Paul made it easier.

"Hey you, c'mere," Paul invited. He drew me into a shadow next to Mom's climbing clematis and lifted my chin, kissing me tenderly at first, and then the pressure increased, and I felt his tongue pushing my lips open as they explored my teeth and tongue. I jerked back, but he pulled me against him again. He was hard, and my nipples responded, jutting outward and becoming highly sensitive. Before I knew it, he had three fingers down the front of my sundress and was massaging my nipple. It felt wonderful and I couldn't help but lean in closer. I wanted more of the same. I heard him chuckle.

Paul gave me another deep kiss before saying, "That's enough for you tonight, missy. I'm going to take my time with you," he added and broke off, gave me a wink and disappeared around the house. I heard his truck start and then he was gone.

I picked up my shoes from the grass where I'd left them and let myself in the back door. I felt like humming as I went up the staircase to my room, but that would wake Mom and Dad and I didn't want to hear any more of that.

* * *

Paul became my shadow that summer. He texted me good morning and sent red kisses at bedtime. It was hard not to be flattered. Those brown eyes always regarded me with mocking humor and I found myself saying things just to make him laugh. He took me to the carnival that came to town and I pretended to be scared in the Ferris wheel so he would bury my face in his chest. I memorized his scent and gave him my full attention.

We went everywhere and each night when he brought me home, he made sure it was after dark, so we could sit in the car in privacy, kissing and touching. I loved his touch and wanted more. He was breaking down the wall I'd built so carefully around myself.

"I think I'm falling in love," I told Patsy who had stopped by one afternoon after she got off work at the library.

"Be careful. He's got a trail of broken hearts," she'd warned me.

I didn't want to say, "I'm different," but that's what was going through my head at the time. I felt invincible. Mom and Dad liked him, and he had a standing invitation to dinner. Dad loved to show off his barbecue skills and Paul carefully admired them aloud, forever endearing him to my parents. I saw them exchange winks and felt my dream move to Chicago slipping from my hands.

* * *

Paul was over, and Dad had outdone himself with

barbecued chicken. Paul had been drinking a few beers and the mood was jovial. After dinner, the mosquitos came for their share and Mom and Dad went inside, leaving Paul and I in the canopied swing.

"Let's get out of here, shall we? Let's take my truck down to the lake and go swimming. I've got the camper on it—we can make a little fire, roast some marshmallows, and I've got beer."

"Beer?"

"Hey, you're an adult now. Your folks even went to bed and by the sounds of it, they could care less where you are, huh?"

He made a very good point and I didn't want to lie on my bed on this warm evening and listen to my mother's giggles. A swim in the lake sounded wonderful.

"Let me get my suit." I pulled away and started toward the door.

"Hey! No, no, you don't need that. We'll go in our birthday suits."

I must have stiffened because I saw caution cross his face. "It's dark there, Gwen. No one will see us, and it will be our little secret."

I gave it one haphazard thought and nodded. "Okay, but just this once."

He didn't give me a chance to change my mind. He leaned down and kissed me again, fondled my nipple once more and tugged me toward his truck. He was right; there was a house on its back. How curious.

It turned out the lake he had in mind was about five miles outside of town. It was a so-so fishing lake and small enough that they didn't allow outboards—strictly an oar lake. He grabbed a blanket from the camper and we found a place beyond the bushes where there were no errant fishhooks embedded in the narrow sandy rim.

Paul handed me a cigarette and I shrugged. *Why not? This can be my wild night before I take on life,* I thought and took a puff, choking on the smoke. If that was what smoking was all about, they could keep it. My throat was on fire and I grabbed the beer from his hand and took three deep gulps before it burned my throat, amplifying the cigarette.

"You like it?" he asked.

"Not really, but hey, I need to try everything once, right?"

"That's my girl," he said, and his teeth gleamed in the moonlight. I loved it when he called me his girl.

"Woah, that thing made me dizzy," I complained mildly as the world began spinning.

"Just float with it," he told me, watching my eyes.

"Float?"

"Haven't you ever smoked pot?"

I froze. "Oh, God, no. Was that...?"

He was nodding and smiling, and his summer-tanned face made his teeth brighter than before.

"You ready to go swimming?"

I felt like I wanted to lie down. My tummy was turning over, I felt hot and dizzy enough to corkscrew into the damp ground. "I guess—that's why we came, right?"

"That's right, darlin'. Come here and let me help you."

I nodded. I wanted help. Paul began by tugging the pink sundress over my head. This freed my breasts. The spaghetti straps wouldn't hide a bra. He stood back, and I heard a low whistle.

"What? What's wrong?"

"Not a thing, darlin'. Not a single thing. God, you're gorgeous!"

"Oh." I was feeling awkward and more than a little hazardous. "Well, let's get into the water."

He caught my arm as I tried to pass by him. "Not so fast. There's more," he said and knelt before me.

I felt his fingers inside my panty waist and then there was cool air as he lowered them to the ground. I heard him draw in his breath. I was feeling confused. This wasn't me. *I don't do these things. I can't think straight.* I could feel a panic building inside me.

"Hey, I changed my mind. I don't want to swim."

"Oh, that's okay. You don't have to. What's wrong, darlin'?"

Oh! There was the other endearment he used with me and it made me melt every time. I looked down at my nakedness with a sort of odd detachment. *That can't be me*, I told myself. "I'm not feeling very good. Hand me my dress, would you? I'm feeling cold and sort of sick."

I watched with swimming eyes as Paul picked up my dress and then stood, scooping me into his arms as he rose.

"Hey!"

"Shhh... I'm just taking you into the camper. You can lie down until you feel better. You don't have to go swimming. Just take a little nap until you're more yourself, huh?"

It sounded so good, but something was still troubling me. I felt like someone else. I nodded and felt the warmth as he opened the camper door and carried me inside. He settled me onto a bunk that was quite comfortable. "I think I'm going to be sick."

"Oops, let me get you a pot or something, but I think you'll be just fine. Just lie there and close your eyes."

I did as he told me and didn't complain when he laid a cool cloth over my eyes.

"Shhh... now then, I'm going to lie here next to you and just stroke your arm. You'll feel more comfortable, I promise."

I felt the weight of his body on the mattress next to me. He was warm. It was nice. His finger began stroking my arm and it sent goosebumps down the length of me. Then the fingers moved to stroke my nipples, one at a time. I shivered with delight. I felt my legs being parted and then he was on top of me.

"No!" screamed something sensible that was overcoming the beer and pot. I knew it was wrong. "No, get off me!" I pushed at him.

"Oh, c'mon darlin'. You're my girl, aren't you? You want some stranger to be your first? Anyway, you know I'm not going to let anything happen to you."

"Paul, I don't want to get pregnant. I'm not on the pill or anything." The beer and pot were having their way with me. I wanted to feel him, but my little girl resistance was screaming at me to stop.

"Don't worry. It will feel good and I promise, I'll be safe." I felt him pull back a little and heard a snap. "See? I put on a condom. No risk and nothing to this. You'll love it. Just relax and lie there. Shhh..."

There was pain, sharp and sudden as he entered me. I tried to push him off and roll away, but his weight was over me like a cement shroud. He began pumping and it pressed into my tummy. I turned my head to one side and vomited. The sour smell didn't seem to bother him. If anything, he sped up and then with a groan, stiffened and arched backward. I took advantage of that pause to shove hard and he fell onto the floor, and likely into the vomit. Grabbing my dress, I pushed past him and blindly felt for the door. It finally fell open.

I drew in great gasps of the fresh air. "Take me home!" I screamed as I pulled my sundress over my head.

"What the hell?" he stumbled out of the camper, pulling on his pants. "Stop screaming!"

"Take-me-home!" I screamed again.

"Okay, okay, get into the truck."

I went around to the passenger side, opened the door and climbed up into the cab, huddling against the door with my eyes closed. "Just drive me home, quickly," I whispered fiercely through gritted teeth.

"What's the matter, darlin'? Didn't it feel good?"

"No, it hurt."

He chuckled a little. "It's always like that your first time, but believe me, it gets better and better. It won't be long before you'll be pulling at me."

I considered his words and the realization of what I'd just done sent thuds of horror into my stomach. Paul drove me home and as soon as he turned into the drive, I bolted from the passenger door and ran to the house, leaving Paul sitting in the driveway. Mom and Dad's window was dark, and the door locked. They evidently thought I was in bed. I dragged the ladder from the side of the shed and climbed up to my own window. I'd left it open to allow cool air and although it took kicking in the screen, I managed to get inside. I was lucky enough to have my own bath. I turned on the hot water and sat in a huddle on the shower floor, letting the water pour over me. I didn't want to remember anything. All I wanted was sleep.

* * *

Paul called that next day, but I wouldn't take the call. I needed time to think. I wanted to move to Chicago, to begin a new life, maybe even do some modeling. It had been my dream. Now I was heavily into Paul and I knew the previous night would be the first of many nights if I let it. It would be too easy to give up my dream and maybe even marry Paul and stay in Brookfield. I wasn't ready to give up so quickly, though. I texted him. "**Give me some space—I have to think.**"

"**Don't take too long**," he texted back.

That wasn't what I wanted to hear. I guess I wanted understanding, or maybe even a commitment. Patsy's words about the trail of broken hearts came back to me. I made up my mind to keep my distance for the time being, so I avoided his calls.

Six weeks later I left the doctor's office, shaking like a leaf. I tapped Paul's number in my phone's missed calls. I'd never opened one.

"Hello?" His voice was a little different than before.

"Paul, it's Gwen. I'm pregnant."

There was a long pause. "No, shit?"

"You told me you used a condom."

Silence again.

"Did you?"

"Don't remember but doesn't matter if I did. It obviously didn't work."

"What are we going to do?" *What did he mean he didn't remember? How could he not remember something that important?*

Another long pause. "Calm down. Calm down now. Look, there's something important I've got to do, but I'll come by tomorrow or Wednesday and we can talk about options."

I disconnected without another word, got into my car and like a zombie, drove home and went to bed, pleading a headache. The next day there was no call from Paul, nor the day after that. I tried his cell, but he didn't pick up. I called Patsy, hoping she'd know where he lived. *How could I not even know where he lived?* She gave me directions and fifteen minutes later I was on his front porch. I rang the bell. A woman answered, and I saw where Paul got his beautiful brown eyes.

"Is Paul here?" I asked.

"No, dear, he's not. We've just returned from the bus terminal. Paul has joined the Army."

Chapter 1

Coulter

I listened as Mason Derry, my attorney, read the accusations contained in the complaint filed against me and my company, Stillman Enterprises. I was twirling the platinum and onyx ring on my right hand; a habit when I was concentrating on something important. "So, what does all that mean?" I asked him.

"Well, in simplest terms, you're being sued for negligence. It is your legal responsibility, as employer, to protect your employees from an unreasonable risk of harm."

"I wasn't even aware anyone had been hurt. Who are we talking about here?"

"His name is James Winkler. He listed his job title as general worker and his duties included sourcing and transferring needed materials from the ground storage up the structure as ordered."

"What went wrong?" I would be the first to admit that building construction on high-rises was dangerous work and I wanted to take immediate measures to be sure no one else would be hurt.

"He claims to have fallen out of a job site elevator

because the gate didn't lock."

"How far did he fall?"

Mason scanned the document and looked at me over his reading glasses. "Four feet."

"You're kidding, right?" I felt the anger rising inside. The guy was clearly out to ruin my reputation or get a big pay-off because he knew I would protect myself with my money.

"I am not. He sustained a broken ankle."

"Mason, you know what the guy is trying to do..."

"I know. I'll answer the complaint and delay it as long as possible."

"No! No delays. Push it through. Get some people on it on our end and bring in everyone on the site that day. I want depositions from everyone."

"It won't be cheap."

"My reputation isn't either," I growled and swiveled the chair so my back was to him. I was done with that conversation.

Mason spoke from the doorway. "You got someone to handle the PR on this?"

"I'll take care of it myself."

I gave Mason five minutes to clear the building and then I got out of my chair and walked to the parking garage where my Mercedes was waiting. Shortly thereafter, I was wearing a hard hat on the job site in question. The foreman on shift showed me where the supposed negligence took place. "I want this inspected immediately and if there's anything wrong, have it fixed. Before you do anything, contact Mason so it doesn't look like we're trying to cover anything up. No one uses this elevator until that's been resolved, got that?" I pointed to it and looked at him hard. "You know anything about this? Were you on shift that day?"

The foreman, Pete Timmer, flushed and I could see he didn't want to tell me something.

"What is it?" I demanded.

He shook his head. "Nothing, sir, nothing. I'll take care of it."

I cocked my head. "Timmer, if I find out that you've held something from me, connected to this or not, you're history, you got that? You're either a member of my team or not."

He scuffed one foot into the gravel and wiped his brow. Guilt was written all over him. He looked over his shoulder. I finally caught on.

"Timmer, I'll be back in my office in fifteen minutes. I want to see you there in thirty. Send everyone home early but don't dock their pay." Without another word, I turned and left, tossing my hardhat into the back seat of the Mercedes.

Liz had just brought me a fresh cup of coffee when Timmer was in the outer office, waiting. I motioned through the glass wall for him to come in. "Sit down."

He was highly uncomfortable, and it had nothing to do with his concrete-caked boots and my Persian carpets. "Mr. Stillman, I got no proof. Just a suspicion. I can't get fired over this—the wife is about to have our fourth and..."

"You won't be fired unless you've done something worth being fired over. Concealing problems from me could be counted as one of those, by the way."

He was pale and shuffling his feet beneath the chair.

"Damnit! What is it?"

"Okay, okay," he held out his hand to calm me down. "See... there are delays on the site every so often. Someone doesn't count inventory and we have to wait on some material, or they run into a problem on one thing that slows down everything behind it..."

"Go on..." My voice was intentionally stern. This was a union town and I didn't need their shit on top of everything else.

"Well, the guys get bored and sometimes they sneak off between some piles and shoot dice and pass the bottle. Especially on cold days, you know?"

I sat forward in my chair. "Are you telling me that the workmen are gambling and drinking on the job?"

He winced. "It sounds worse than it is."

"Oh, really?" I was losing my calm and felt the heat rising into my brain. "Was this guy, this Winkler—was he drinking that day?"

"I honestly don't know. I wasn't on until later in the day. McNamara was covering for me; I had a root canal. So, I can't say that I saw him drinking."

"Where are they getting the booze?" This was a major OSHA offense and they could shut down my building sites over this kind of thing.

"You know...they bring it with them. A flask, the back pocket inside their overalls."

"Timmer, are *you* drinking or gambling on the site?"

"Me? Hell, no. Even if I wanted to, it would be suicide.

There's guys who don't like me, you know? They'd be the first to rat on me and my job would be done, or I could wind up taking a tumble off a girder. No, I do my drinking on my own time, at home."

I believed him. It made sense. I had to be careful how I handled this information. With inspectors and lawyers sniffing around, if I made it obvious I was confiscating booze, they'd hang me even higher.

"Now look, Timmer. You get the other supervisors together and I want it circulated, word of mouth to every single person who sets foot on that site in my employ... There will be no more drinking, no more gambling and no drugs or guns. Got that? I want it as clean as a nunnery on that site. Anyone caught will answer to me, and that won't be pretty."

I didn't need to be specific. Most of the guys had heard of my reputation as a hardass and that would be enough. Timmer leapt up from his chair. "Yes, sir, thank you, sir."

"You're back in that chair in one week with a progress report, you hear me?" He nodded, and I waved him out.

My private cell buzzed. It was Mason. "What is it?" I answered brusquely.

"Sorry, but the word got out. All your construction

permits have been suspended pending an outcome of the hearing."

"What? All of them? Other sites?"

"I'm on it."

"What are you going to do?"

"I'm re-organizing you under one holding company. That separates your other assets. You may have to find some CEOs to sit in your place for a while, but we'll keep the show running."

"Just *do* it."

I hated getting stabbed in the back. I absolutely hated it.

Chapter 2

Gwen

"Oh, Gwen, you look absolutely awesome in that shade of blouse beneath that suit." Bitsy was sitting on the flowered slipper chair, bouncing Carrie on her lap.

"Honestly? You really think so?"

Bitsy nodded with an exaggerated motion. "Absolutely. Of course, I couldn't pull off that look. I don't have enough meat on my bones. But you? I'd kill for your body."

"Oh, don't be silly. You have your own sweet shape. It's just a matter of learning to dress so that you accentuate your positives and play down the negatives."

"Yeah, but you don't have any negatives as far as I can see," Bitsy pointed out, kissing the top of Carrie's head.

"You think the color is right for me?"

"Oh, don't be silly. It matches your eyes exactly. You chose it on purpose, I know you did." Bitsy's voice was becoming a little strident. She was better at single word responses. When you asked her opinion, it seemed to make her nervous and everything went downhill from there.

"Well, okay, if you say so. This job is really important to me, you know?"

"Of course. It's like your dream job, right? Who wouldn't want to work for Blaze House? It's like the nicest dress shop in town and only caters to women with a ton of money, let me tell you." Bitsy's envy was obvious in her face.

"Well, you would know better than I. You've lived here longer. Listen, I'm grateful for you asking your friend to get me an interview. Those modeling classes I took only take you so far, you know? At some point, you have to know someone who knows someone to make use of them." I was trying to make her feel better.

Bitsy bounced Carrie harder, almost to the point for the little one was ready to cry. I could tell Bitsy was worked up. I took Carrie from her and made the pretense of cuddling her, just to get Bitsy to calm down. "Don't mention it. She owed me a couple favors, anyway."

"Will you be okay here with Carrie alone?" I was having second thoughts. This could all fall apart if Bitsy wasn't up to taking care of my baby.

"Well, I'd better be. If you get this job, no, let me change that—w*hen* you get this job. I'm looking after her during the day, so she and I had better get used to one another really quickly." Bitsy took her back from me. Carrie's little finger when into her mouth and then she reached up and touched the tip of Bitsy's nose.

* * *

Her name was Metallica, obviously the result of poor judgment on her mother's behalf. I felt awkward even asking for her when I arrived for my interview. I was shown to an ultra-modern office on the second floor of the building. I climbed the crimson carpeted staircase, looking down at the displays and racks of beautiful clothing and equally beautiful women. It was as if I was walking in my own dream. The girl who showed me to Metallica's office tapped on the door and then stood back and gave me a solemn look. It was as if she were showing me into the den of a lion. The woman at the desk looked up, and I instantly understood.

"Thank you for being prompt," she said as she stood, towering over me by at least foot. I imagined that her ancestors were those solemn, majestic people who ran for days without stopping across the Serengeti. Her cheekbones were to die for and her slender, aquiline nose gave her one of the most beautiful profiles I thought I'd ever seen. "I am Metallica, and I assume you are Gwen?"

I nodded and held out my hand. "It's nice to meet you," I said softly, thoroughly intimidated.

"Please, sit down." I obliged and took a few brief seconds to breathe in the atmosphere of her office. It suited her perfectly, which made me believe she had probably designed it herself. It was flawless good taste, original concept and could have only existed in a magazine like *Architectural Digest.* She cleared her throat and had my full attention immediately.

"I am sorry, but it doesn't appear as though you have had much experience." Her elegant eyes were studying my reaction.

"You're right, but it is proportionate to my age. I've done some homework regarding Blaze and I know that your employees tend to be younger than twenty-five. As you can see on my resume, I have taken some fashion merchandising and modeling classes and I've been lucky enough to get a few modeling assignments. I believe your customers come because you offer a fantasy world. Your clothing is without equal and when a woman is looking for a fantasy, I believe she wants to be treated like a queen. You're right, I am very young, but that also means that I don't offer them any competition. Let them see me as their handmaiden, if you will."

"An interesting perspective, and very creative." She looked at my resume once more and then pushed her chair back from the desk, crossing unbelievably long legs that only reaffirmed my suspicions of her ancestry. I'd often been told I had beautiful legs, but mine were stunted compared to her length. "Assuming you were to come to work here at Blaze, how do you picture your future?"

"There are things about me that really don't belong on a resumé," I told her. "If you knew me, you would know that I'm ambitious and focused. Some people might even say a little too focused, but I question whether that's even possible. Although it will sound quite juvenile, I'll tell you honestly, I come from a small town and I've seen everything it has to offer. I want more excitement in my life. I want to speak with intelligent people about intelligent subjects; I want to see and experience a way of life that I never could have found in my hometown. If that means that I begin here, with you, at Blaze, I would consider that part of the dream already realized. Your customers are successful people, by nature. That's where I belong. So, to answer your question, Blaze could be the beginning of my life, or it could be the focus of my life. I preferred the latter, to be honest."

Metallica laughed, a deep throaty sound that was half mocking and half knowing. "You remind me very much of myself at your age," she said. "Which is not to say I'm that much older than you are," she pointed out quickly, her eyebrows rising defiantly. I did the wisest thing I could think of and kept my mouth shut.

"I think I have seen enough. I believe you will need a wardrobe that showcases your body style. I will expect you to report next Monday morning and you will have training on your first day, followed by four days of shadowing my top salesgirl. Be invisible but learn, if you understand me."

I nodded, my heart pounding that it had been this easy.

"You may go now. I will call downstairs and have an account opened in your name. Please choose some basic items as foundations, and then throw your own personal flair. You must look like you belong at Blaze. We will deduct a small amount each week from your salary to pay for the clothing, although you will receive a 60% discount."

I could hardly believe my ears. I had just landed a job at one of the most exclusive and admired dress shops in the entire city and was getting not only a healthy discount, but the opportunity to enter a world I could have only dreamed of back in Brookfield. As I practically stumbled back down the staircase, it suddenly occurred to me that we had never negotiated my wage. It was the first of many things I learned when dealing with people of money. The first most important was that you never discussed it. It was simply understood that integrity and fairness were involved. In other words, should it become public knowledge that Blaze paid their clerks a substandard wage, the store would lose credibility and therefore, customers. They also included in their message to their customers that you got what you paid for. That was how they justified their outrageous prices. Likewise, if they paid a substandard wage, their employees would reflect that. This gave me a certain sense of pride and as I arrived at the foot of the stairs, a woman came up to me and introduced herself as Christine.

"Metallica asked me to show you around and get you set up," she said in a kind, but neutral voice.

"Thank you," I told her, my knee shaking slightly at the realization of what was going to be my future. Christine took me on a brief, but thorough walk-through of the store. She pointed out the general concept of the store's layout, pairing displays with products in various sizes nearby. It was quite ingenious, actually. Much of that I had learned in merchandising classes, but each store had their own methods. They tracked customer movement throughout the store, noting what caught someone's eye and what entice them to pick up the merchandise for a firsthand touch. There was a science as well as the psychology behind it. They moved the customer through the store, propelling them by their own desire to investigate the newest object of fascination in their path.

When we completed the tour, Christine asked me to follow her into a small employee room behind the red curtain. There she gave me forms to complete and a store credit card. "You have carte blanche, obviously, since you will ultimately be paying for everything you pick out today. The 60% discount is a one-time opportunity, so I would make most of it. After today, you get the standard 20% discount on employee purchases, and you can only use those for yourself, not as gifts for others. So, here you go. I'm sure there were few things that caught your eye as we walked around. When you're done, catch my attention and I'll run you through the checkout personally. Welcome to Blaze and now it's time to go have fun." She smiled broadly and swept her arm outward to indicate that I should get started. I felt an exhilaration that I could only compare to completing a flawless cheerleading routine and hearing the fans applauding in appreciation. This was my chance to strut my stuff and I couldn't wait to get started.

I was like a kid in a candy store. I knew that I had decent taste, and I had learned more while I was in school. That said, even da Vinci would have been challenged to paint the Mona Lisa with only four colors of paint. I tried to keep it very low-key, although everything inside me screamed to become a Walmart shopper dragging three or four cars behind me as I piled in clothes.

I took Metallica's advice and began with the basics. I chose foundation garments such as pencil skirts and tailored slacks in several different dark colors. There were vests and jackets to match and I added these onto my pile. Then I wandered into the tops with sweaters and blouses and finally into dresses where I chose my first little black basic dress ever. I struck out for lingerie and then casual clothing, although I kept this to a minimum because I couldn't wear that to work. Lucky for me, they had shelves and shelves filled with beautiful shoes, very expensive shoes. I avoided the traditional brands and went for elegant, but more practical styles. After all, I knew I had to pay for this eventually, but I did need it to start and I would never get a discount like this again. I think it was an hour and a half later before I finally wound up at the counter and caught Christine's eye. She was grinning as she walked toward me. "Everyone does the same thing," she laughed. "Don't worry, they have special sales for us from time to time even though they don't tell you about it. And sometimes, when you do a really good job, I'll give you a bonus discount as a reward."

My eyes must have lit up at the idea. "My paycheck is going to be zero each week," I pointed out and she laughed as she nodded and tallied up my purchases. When I finally left the store, I had so many bags I needed to borrow a luggage cart. I found my car and began unloading all my purchases into the trunk and then returned the card before driving back toward the apartment that Bitsy and I shared with my daughter.

I could hardly wait to get home and tell Bitsy my good news. I walked through the door to find her on the sofa, sound asleep. Carrie was in her crib. "Mama missed you sweetie," I told her as I picked her up and held her at my shoulder. "Did Bitsy go to sleep on you?"

I carried her into the next room and put her in her carrier, so I could watch her while I made dinner. She knew what I was doing and started fussing. I wondered how long it had been since Betsy fed her. I was so excited that I purposefully slammed the silverware drawer. It worked.

Bitsy came around the kitchen doorway, poking her head in as her eyes blinked heavily with sleep. "When did you get home?"

"Just a few minutes ago. Do you remember what time you fed Carrie?"

"It hasn't been that long, maybe an hour."

I decided not to interrogate her any further. It was obvious she'd been asleep for quite a while, but Carrie was quite safe in her crib. Bitsy and I had an unusual, but very practical roommate arrangement. She worked nights as a 911 operator and now I would work days. We shared the childcare, the utilities, the food and part of the rent. I gave her sort of a discount based on babysitting and it worked well for both of us. I had some money saved and then there were my graduation gifts back from Brookfield. Mom and Dad had thrown in a nice sum in lieu of sending me to college. I think they felt sorry for me that I'd gotten pregnant. In a small town like Brookfield, that sort of thing was frowned upon even though this was no longer the 60s. Mom and Dad helped me keep things very quiet and as soon as Carrie was born, I started modeling school. I was proof that you never had to give up your dreams, no matter how impossible they might seem. I'd never heard a word from

Paul and looking back, I was glad. It was hard enough to get where I wanted to go on my own with a small child. If he'd come back and wanted into our lives, there was no way I would be where I was at that moment.

"Sit down, you won't believe what happened today."

Bitsy looked over at the clock. "I've only got a half hour before I have to leave for work," she pointed out.

I nodded. "I'm just making us burgers and they'll be ready in a few minutes. But listen, that's not the news."

"What's the news?"

"I got a job." I waited for her sleepy head to catch up with what I was saying.

"No! You didn't! Are you talking about Blaze? They hired you? That's unbelievable, I'm so excited for you!" She leapt out of her chair and threw her arms around me from the back. As shy as she was, Bitsy had a soft place in her heart for Carrie and me. We were family. She looked after me like my own mother would.

"Absolutely, I start on Monday. And that's not the best part. They let me have a shopping spree at sixty percent off and you should see the things I bought. Of course, I'll have to pay for them gradually, out of my check, but who cares? It's a wardrobe and that was one of my biggest worries."

"Oh, there's no way I can look at it all before I have to leave. Promise me you'll leave it all in bags just as it is and when I get home, you can put on your own fashion show for me?"

"Okay, okay, you sure know how to torture a girl."

"Oh, don't start feeling sorry for yourself. You can use this time to get some sleep. Carrie didn't have a very long nap and I'm sure she'll ready for bed as soon as you give her dinner."

"Oh? I thought you just fed her a few minutes ago?" I rolled my eyes and nodded as I turned back to the skillet.

"Oh. Well, that was when I was still half asleep. No, she needs to eat again before she goes to bed. Let me run into the bedroom and throw on my clothes for tonight. I'll be back in a minute and eat. I can't wait to hear about it when I come home."

I could hear the excitement in her voice. Bitsy tended to live vicariously through me. I suspicioned that she had not been very popular in school and while that made no difference to me, she followed my every movement like a parent. If I began to wear my hair a certain way, eventually she did the same. She almost looked after Carrie almost as much as I did, which was only another advantage to rooming with her, of course.

We ate our burgers quickly and as Bitsy grabbed her sack lunch and her purse, she headed toward the door and said to me over her shoulder, "Oh, by the way, someone delivered that envelope for you. I had to sign for it." She pointed to the small table by the door. "See you later."

I looked at the envelope from where I sat. My stomach instantly turned. I lived in constant fear that Paul would show up and try to come after me. He might have a change of heart and have actually grown up while he was away and decided that he wanted to see Carrie. I couldn't let that happen. I dreaded the day that I had to explain to her where her daddy was. I'd come up with all sorts of scenarios in my mind, but I had always been one to go for the truth, no matter how lousy that would make her feel. It wasn't about her, I would explain. It was about me, but mostly, it was about Paul.

Sighing, I got up and retrieved the envelope, slitting it open with a kitchen knife. It looked very official and I saw that it was issued from the court system. My heart plummeted until I began reading and realized it had nothing to do with Carrie, Paul, or anyone, but me. It was a summons for jury duty. I groaned. How could I take off work for jury duty when I hadn't even started yet? I read the letter through and saw that I was supposed to report in forty-eight hours. I would just have to go down to the courthouse and tell them they'd have to excuse me. I had an infant and I needed that job badly. They just would have to let me out of it.

Chapter 3

Coulter

Wearing a tailored charcoal colored suit, immaculate cuffs and collar that accentuated my tan, I sat completely relaxed, if not even somewhat defiant in my seat at the defendant's table. It was intentional. I wanted everyone to see that I wasn't the least concerned with the proceedings. I even saw a couple of people sketching me—likely from some of the media who weren't exactly my fans. Mason sat quietly next to me, a laptop in a folder with papers before him.

"How long do you think this will take?" I asked.

"It shouldn't be long," Mason reassured me. "Now that the jury selection is complete, I will ask the judge to dismiss the case based on the evidence we've provided. Between you and me, he'd be a fool to do anything else. He's up for reelection and crucifying us is not going to earn him any brownie points."

I nodded as a door to one side opened and people began filing in and filling the jury box. I couldn't help but notice one very young woman who took her seat in the second row. It was obvious by the look on her face as she glared at me that she was not happy to be there. My money carried a great deal of weight around town and it wasn't always possible to see who might have a problem with me. It was one of the downsides of development; turning some people's lives upside down as you move toward the greater good. Some people took it personally. I saw it as a way of revitalizing Chicago's downtown, in a way that would keep it alive, unlike its sister city, Detroit, just three hundred miles away. Keeping the downtown vital provided good paying jobs, safe places to live and entertainment. These brought in tax dollars that the city's motors running. It was a win-win, but I had to admit that from time to time someone got run over in the process. I tried to anticipate those situations and send representatives to help relocate those who were adversely affected. Sometimes they just didn't want to leave.

I assumed she may be one of them. I was disappointed, because she was just my type. Wearing a deep red, expensive suit, she held her head high in a way that told me she was used to getting her way. I liked confidence in a woman. She crossed her legs and I held my breath in that sweet second that her knees were parted. I could even feel myself hardening, despite my precarious position. Her blonde hair was braided into a bun at the top of her elegant neck and from my distance, I could see her eyes were unusual; dark and mysterious. She leaned forward to pick up a pencil from the floor and I glimpsed a deep valley between full breasts in the V-neckline of her suit. Damn! She was not on my side and she was exactly the person I wanted in my corner—if not on my lap.

The jury was seated, the judge entered, and Mason

immediately made a motion to drop the charges. The judge called for the prosecutor and Mason to approach the bench and when they turned, I knew victory was mine. The prosecutor wore a sour look and glared in my direction. Mason had done his work well. He had evidence that the injured worker had been drinking heavily all morning on the day of the accident. He'd neglected to shut the gate that would have kept him safely inside. He also stumbled in his drunkenness, sliding through the opening onto the ground below. Subpoenaed records from the ER where he had been treated indicated his blood alcohol level was three times the legal limit. Indeed, the victim was guiltier than I could've ever been. He endangered the lives of every man on that site as he operated equipment and make judgment calls in a drunken state of mind. The judge knew it was a waste of time and saw his way out. The prosecuting attorney saw a potential negligence disaster for his client and without a job, there was no way the attorney would ever see a penny. The gavel came down and I stood to shake Mason's hand and draw a deep breath of relief.

I looked toward the jury and saw the blonde staring at me, a look that told me she was not only angry with me, but with the world in general. I wondered what her story was and made it a point to mutter a few words in my assistant's ear. "You see that young lady over there in the dark red suit?" Peter nodded. "Find out who she is—what her story is. She's shooting daggers at me like she'd like to roast me on a spit."

Peter didn't hesitate but left immediately as the jury filed out of the courtroom. I was relieved the trial had been so brief—I had details to see to, the first of which was getting my permits reactivated and the men back to work. I'd kept them all on full salary pending the outcome of the trial, but I had time commitments on the contracts. It was time to get back to work. That said, I couldn't get the blonde out of my mind.

Chapter 4

Gwen

I unlocked the door and tossed my purse and shoes on the chair by the door. Bitsy looked up. "Hard day?"

"You have no idea," I answered, scooping up Carrie to cuddle while I unwound from my long Saturday at the store.

"I made dinner," Bitsy threw in, but from the smell of what was coming from the kitchen, I wasn't sure I wanted any. She was not known for her cooking; a fact she readily admitted. "It's a sort of skillet burrito but I used cornbread mix 'cause we were out of tortillas."

"You know what? Why don't you save that for your lunch tomorrow? I got paid today and I'm going to take us out on the town tonight to celebrate. I saw Mrs. Heathrow on the way up and she'd be glad to watch Carrie."

Bitsy dropped the book she was reading. "Really? You're buying? Wow, I haven't been out to have fun in a long, long time."

"Sure, I mean it. You know, I've been meaning to ask you. Doesn't your job get to you? I mean, all those emergencies, that stress, the sad stories?"

"Nope," she answered, unfolding her bent leg from beneath the other as she stood up and stretched. "I figure for every sad ending; my job makes it possible for there to be a dozen happy ones."

I nodded. "A good way to look at it. Listen, I'm going to take Carrie down to Mrs. Heathrow. Why don't you take your turn in the shower and then I'll take mine—if you leave me any hot water, that is," I grinned slyly. "Hey, why don't you call some of our friends and tell them we're going down to Pier 101. Maybe they'd like to meet us there?"

"Wow, this sounds like a whole party."

"Why not? Oh, but Bitsy... I'm only treating you and myself. The others are on their own, okay?"

"Hmmm... sounds like you're not quite the Miss Moneybags you'd like me to think. You sure you can do this?"

"I'm sure. Go on, get in the water. I'll be back up in about ten minutes." I packed a quick bag for Carrie, tossing in a couple of bottles, diapers, a change of jammies and her favorite teething ring and cuddly doll. Her dark eyes watched me, and I think she sensed I was going to leave because she started crying. I picked her up and loved on her, rocking her until she drifted off to sleep in my arms. Grabbing the bag for my shoulder, I crept downstairs and tapped on Mrs. Heathrow's door. I handed her the bag and then Carrie. "I'll bring down the porta-crib in a few minutes on my way out. She'll be fine on her blanket on the floor until I get back. Thank you!" I added and took the stairs two at a time.

I laid out some leather leggings and a new, low-cut top I'd picked up at work in a weak moment. Bitsy slept on the pull-out since we needed a room with a door for Carrie and that's where I slept, too. "Use your vanity?" she asked lightly as she passed me and didn't wait for an answer. It almost felt like a holiday.

After my shower, I quickly dried my hair and pulled out my make-up. I used the sparkle eye shadow—something I couldn't possibly wear to the more sedate atmosphere at the store. I grabbed the porta-crib and my handbag, and we were off!

"I didn't get a chance to ask. Were you able to find anyone who wanted to join us?" Bitsy and I were walking to Pier 101. We were only a few blocks away and walking so that we didn't have to watch how much we drank. Our neighborhood was safe, if a bit ragged looking.

"Oh, yes, Tim said he's coming and bringing somebody. Marcy will bring the girls as soon as they're out of work, which should be about anytime now. But you and I both know that the idea is to meet new people," she said, winking at me.

"My idea is to have a relaxing evening out, and I appreciate knowing a few people there. It's always awkward to get up and dance when you don't have a partner."

We arrived at Pier 101, a short line had already begun to form outside the double doors. There was a bouncer checking for the usual; guns, drugs, hidden flasks. When he came to me, he just smiled and patted me on the rump. I drew in my breath, but then consider he could've patted a whole lot more. I had to remember that he was protecting me as well as everyone else inside. "You have fun, now, you hear?" he said, winking at me. I hoped my night was going to be a little more interesting than being hit on by the bouncer.

Inside, dance music practically made the walls shudder. Spectrums of light bounced off ceiling, floors and walls, making the atmosphere feel frenetic. Bitsy went to scope out a table while I went to get us a couple of drinks. They didn't have a cover charge here, but you were expected to have a drink. Bitsy liked the colored, frothy drinks. Those had always sent me to the bathroom to lose it before the night was over, so I chose Scotch and water. I hated the taste, which prompted me to sip slowly. That way I stayed sober enough to know what I was doing but just tipsy enough to enjoy doing it.

I found Bitsy at a large table, surrounded by the friends she promised were coming. I had to admit it was much better being part of the group. “Oh, that looks just delicious,” Bitsy squealed, taking the pink drink in a margarita glass I held out to her. “You always know just what I like.” She spilled a little in her lap and her mouth formed a guilty *O* and then she broke out in giggles. That was normal Bitsy.

I sat down, and we started a shouting conversation between us. Some of the people I didn’t know, but others I just hadn’t seen for quite a while. Of course, in my case, quite a while wasn’t all that long since I’d only recently moved to town. Talking felt like walking against the current, it just didn’t make any sense in this over-the-top atmosphere.

I looked up to see Tim standing next to me. “You want to dance?” he asked, jerking his head in the direction of the dance floor.

I nodded and slid out of the booth, following him.

There are a few things to be said for dance music. It is so unmemorable that when you go home at night, there is no tune running through your head as you try to go to sleep. It is also not romantic. You can dance with a perfect stranger and not feel obligated to touch them. And it is as equally hard to maintain a conversation while dancing as it is sitting in a booth. For all these reasons, I let myself go and let the bass feed my heartbeat.

Tim just smiled at me from time to time and nodded, a friendly gesture that made me feel comfortable with him. I'd suspected he had an interest in me for a while, but he wasn't my type and I certainly wasn't able to party with his crowd. I was a mother and a career woman and those two had to take precedence. The music changed, and I started some new moves, stepping from my left to my right. I came back to forward and saw that Tim was standing to one side, shrugging. In front of me was someone entirely different. To my amazement, it was the man from the trial, the defendant. *How the hell had he gotten there?*

Tim was gesturing with his hand, asking if it was okay that he wanted to sit down. I rolled my eyes and nodded for him to go ahead, not at all happy with the change in dance partner. Despite the overwhelming noise, I asked, "What are you doing here?"

"I came by to dance and saw you out here on the floor. I recognized you as the girl in my jury and I was a little surprised. Quite a coincidence, wouldn't you say?"

I hadn't liked his attitude in the courtroom, so much so that I think I'd already found him guilty before the trial even began. It was probably better that it never came to a jury decision. There was an arrogance about him, as though he expected the world about him. It reminded me of someone, someone who had dealt a major blow to my future. I couldn't be friendly. "I don't remember inviting you."

"Is this a private party?" he taunted me, feigning surprise by jerking his head backward. I saw the muscles in his throat, heavy and strong. Everything about him suggested power.

"This wasn't a coincidence, was it?"

He laughed a little. "No, not really."

"Are you saying you've been following me?"

He stopped dancing then and took me by the hand, pulling me from the dance floor toward the bar in the corner of the room. It was only slightly quieter there but at least you could hold a conversation. "I'll put my cards on the table. I saw you walk into the jury box. I liked your attitude."

"My attitude?"

"You didn't like me, did you?"

He was perceptive, at least. "Well, here comes my cards on the table. No, I didn't like what I saw."

"And what did you see?"

"I saw a man who believed in his own power, dressed in a suit that was costumed to make him look modest and innocent, but his face couldn't hide his disdain for the people and situations around him."

He signaled the bartender, who must've known him because he returned instantly with two glasses of wine. I shook my head and pushed one away. "I have a drink at my table."

"We'll talk first and then I'll take you to your table," he said in a commanding voice.

I could feel the hackles begin to rise but there was something compelling about his presence. Was I falling for that "I'm so powerful" routine?

He sipped his wine and I could see it was an opportunity to think through his next words. "Good girl, you don't pull any punches. That said, I think you might have misread what you saw on my face. The truth is that neither you nor I should have ever been in that room that day. I was being set up. The man who brought suit against me fabricated the story and I have a bad feeling that someone put him up to it."

"So, you were innocent? Isn't that what they all say?"

"Do you automatically assume everyone who walks into a courtroom is guilty?"

I didn't hesitate. "Aren't we all guilty of something? Large or small?"

"What are you guilty of?" He turned and settled both elbows on the bar as if my response would take some thought. His question took my breath for a moment. The words that filled the air between us were like verbal swords, parrying to size up the opponent like two determined fencers.

"Perhaps I was guilty of jumping to a conclusion about you. Would that be fair?"

"That would be fair," he nodded. He took another sip of his wine as though he were looking for his next moves. "You're here alone." It was a statement, not a question.

I could be equally misleading. "No, as a matter of fact, I'm not."

"Ree-aa-lly?" He dragged out the word, evidence of his disbelief. His voice was mesmerizing. It was deep and a little raspy, textured, and emotional. I hadn't noticed from the distance of the jury box that his eyes were a brilliant blue, contrasting with raven's wing black hair. As a blonde, I resented the dumb blonde jokes and it always wished that I had black hair. A part of my womanhood heated up and I realized I was attracted to him. I quickly thought of something else, unwilling to give up my first impression of him. "So, why don't you introduce me to your friends? Let's see if anyone claims you?" he needled me.

"Are you calling me a liar?"

“Of course not. I’d just like to see your date.”

I nodded, pushed the goblet of wine in the bartender’s direction and swiveled the stool so I could bypass the dance floor and walk to my table. Once I got there, I squeezed in next to Tim and wrapped my arm beneath his, laying my cheek on his shoulder. “Tim, this man doesn’t believe you are my date.”

Tim’s face took on a puzzled look. “Well…” I knew I’d made a mistake. Tim had a thing for another guy so there could be nothing but friendship between us. I pinched him beneath the table, hoping he would catch on. He did. “Of course, she’s my date. Did you forget it was my shoulder you tapped on to dance with her?”

The Stillman guy grinned wickedly. “Okay, okay, have it your own way,” he said with a knowing look. We’d made it worse, not believable. He looked toward the entrance and signaled someone. A man walked over to our table. His face was affable, and he certainly didn’t resemble Stillman at all. He was considerably shorter, fair in coloring with a light sprinkle of freckles across his full face. “My friend, William Clark, although friends call him Buddy,” he introduced. Yes, he looked like a Buddy.

Bitsy’s face lit up; there was fresh, untried male in the vicinity! “Hi, Buddy,” she said, going straight for the familiarity jugular. “There’s room here for you next to me.”

To my great surprise, Buddy seemed to like the idea and the people next to Bitsy piled out of the booth to let him take a seat next to her. She grabbed an empty glass, poured beer into it from a pitcher on the table and handed it to him. "So, Buddy, tell me all about yourself." I knew Bitsy had already had too many pink fizzles; she was obviously gregariously drunk.

Stillman looked at me. I suppose he was waiting for a likewise invitation. I ignored him, clung to Tim's arm and studied the dancers. "No?" he asked.

I continued to look past him. "I guess not," he said and dragged a chair from another table to sit somewhat opposite me—just enough to block my view of the dance floor. He signaled a waiter who soon reappeared with bottles of champagne and stemmed flutes for everyone at the table. He was followed by more waiters with trays filled with expensive finger food like shrimp, caviar, small crustless sandwiches and the most delicious-looking squares of some sort of pasta. My tummy growled but I ignored it all and stuck with my nasty Scotch. Stillman just grinned at me as he passed around the food and drink.

"So, Miss Patterson, I wonder if you would share with me, and of course, the group, just what it was that you saw in me that made me your instant enemy?" There were several gasps around the table. He'd bought my own friends away from me and I was steaming.

"You think you're entitled to be right," I said and there was silence at the table as the others waited for his response. It was golden.

"I usually am," he said arrogantly and tossed a shrimp into his mouth with the accuracy of an NBA player slamming the hoop. He was wearing a thick, Norwegian sweater that made his muscled shoulders even broader. Damn that stirring in my tummy!

"What gives you the superiority to think you're always right?" I threw at him.

"No, I mean I usually *am* right. I make it my business to have all the facts and then form an opinion..." he said casually and then added, "...unlike *some* people who jump to conclusions." There was another small gasp around the table and I knew I'd lost point, set and match. I wanted to slap him and then kiss him, in that order. *What was wrong with me?*

Stillman stayed in his place, eating, drinking, and telling stories to the others of his travels around the world. He talked about his father and it was apparent he'd been raised with manners... and with money. He had me trapped and that made me furious. If I ignored him and got up to dance, he'd follow me. If I stayed in my seat, I had to listen with the others because he was certainly monopolizing the conversation. All except for his friend, Buddy. It seemed that

Bitsy had hooked herself a live one because she was chattering in drunken animation and Buddy couldn't take his eyes off her.

"Ms. Patterson, would you care to dance?" Stillman asked, deliberately calling me by my last name. He knew everyone at the table already.

I shook my head and leaned into Tim.

"I see. Well, it appears I've outstayed my welcome," he said smoothly and stood up. He reached into his pocket and pulled out a white card, sliding it across the table until it came to rest against my breasts that slightly topped the table. His fingers lingered, and I could feel my nipples harden. *Damn him*! "Here's my card. Send me a text when you're available," he said with a wink in Tim's direction. "I'll be waiting to hear from you. Buddy?"

"I'll find my own way home, Colt," Buddy called out and Stillman gave him a thumbs-up. He nodded to me and turned away, raising a fingertip to signal a man who was leaning against the wall of the dance club. The man, dressed in a black suit, had an earpiece that glinted in the colored lights. It was obvious he was not there to drink or dance but followed Stillman five paces behind as they left the club.

"Who in the world was that?" Bitsy could hardly contain herself.

I shrugged. "Just the guy on trial. Remember, I told you I had jury duty?"

"That's Colt Stillman. One of the finest guys you could ever hope to know," Buddy chimed in.

Bitsy leaned forward and picked up the card, holding it into the light of the candle at the center of our table. Her mouth formed an *O*. "Do you know who that is?"

I pretended nonchalance. "I told you—he's the guy from the trial."

Bitsy passed the card around the table. "Never mind that. That guy is like a bazillionaire! He owns skyscrapers all over town. He's like the most eligible bachelor there is. How did you happen to run into him?"

"He followed me here." I tried to say it quickly and briefly, so no one would make a big deal out of it, but Bitsy's description was far more interesting than my own explanation.

"Oh, my God, are you kidding? He's interested in you?"

"Is that so hard to believe?" I felt a little insulted that Bitsy thought I was not desirable enough to attract someone like Stillman, but I didn't want to let on that I found him the least bit intriguing.

Tim spoke up. “So, what was this thing about being my date?”

I pushed at his arm and gave them a quick peck on the cheek. “Sorry to spring on you like that. He was trying to pick me up and I wanted him to think that I was with a guy.”

“Well, I am a guy, but I don’t think he bought the idea that I was your date. I could tell by the look in his eyes, he knew you were lying.”

I shrugged again. “Doesn’t matter,” I said nonchalantly as I scanned the room. “You know, Bitsy? I guess I didn’t realize how tired I am. I’m going to go ahead and walk home, but here,” I reached into my purse and pulled out two $20 bills and slid them into her hand. She looked down and nodded.

“Sure you don’t want me to go with you?” I knew she was being polite; she was wrapped all over Buddy.

“No, you stay and have a good time. It’s been a long day. I’m going to grab Carrie and go home to bed.” Bitsy looked immensely relieved and she waved briefly and blew me a kiss. Voices from around the table said goodnight as I picked up my bag, tossed down one more sip of the wretched Scotch and headed out the door. Within an hour, both Carrie and I were sound asleep. Bitsy told me the next morning that as soon as I left, the conversation turned to everyone plotting to get me into Stillman’s hands, including her new friend, Buddy. Didn't people have anything better to do?

Chapter 5

Coulter

What was it about that woman that got under my skin? I don't mean that she irritated me, I mean that I *wanted* her under my skin, with me on top and only blankets over the both of us.

I'd seen beautiful women before, but they knew it. This one, well, she was different. Didn't she see the image she drove into a man's mind? The stunning turquoise eyes? The endless legs and that sweet, yet intelligent innocence that begged me to teach her everything I knew—and I'm not talking about business.

Peter had done his job well. He'd brought me her name, where she lived, details on her roommate and where she worked. She looked the part for a high-class dress shop. *With a shape like hers, she'd bring life to a bedsheet.* I couldn't let myself picture her face without getting hard. It was becoming an issue. I could hardly get through a business meeting without an erection, and that made me lose my concentration and become vulnerable. I had to do something about it.

I knew she wouldn't call or text me. She might not have even taken the card with her. I knew Buddy would put in a good word for me—in fact, I counted on it. Buddy had been on me to find a woman and settle down—if for no better reason than he wouldn't have to be my "date" all of the time and could start a life of his own. I was amazed how friendly he was that night. Normally, he was a bulldog. I knew he wasn't drunk; he never let himself lose control. Surely, it couldn't have been the girl—Bitsy? Was that her name? She seemed scatter-brained, but then it could have been the booze.

I had my hands full with the business, but I was so pre-occupied with Gwen Patterson that I knew I'd have to resolve my infatuation with her before I could return to my normal productivity. I knew the only solution was to let it run its course. I'd been there several times before. I looked at women like business acquisitions. They seemed tantalizing and perfect until I had them; that's when I lost interest and moved on. I knew it was a crappy way to treat women and that's why I seldom got involved and never with someone as clean-thinking and decent as Gwen. She was too easily manipulated and would be a mental crime scene when I moved on. I almost felt like a vampire—wanting someone's lifeblood and yet knowing they would be dead after our encounter. It was unconscionable. But, it was true.

I couldn't do that to her; I couldn't take away that fresh innocence and leave behind cynicism and regrets. I'd sold my soul to the devil to get where I was and now the devil was demanding his due. I had to pay it—not Gwen.

So, I forced myself to put her out of my mind. It was like trying to kick an addiction. *What the hell is the matter with me? I don't even know her; not what she likes or hates, not where she's been before, how she was brought up, what turned her on. I knew nothing.*

That, in effect, was what made her enticing. I'd had enough therapists who found it their solemn duty to explain that to me. I wanted a family, wanted a son or daughter to teach what I'd learned and mastered. There had been women; beautiful, smart creatures who would have made excellent mothers. The cycle repeated itself. They were perfect, they were a commitment, they became flawed in my mind and I'd justified leaving.

I'd sworn off women, but for some niggling reason, Gwen was different. She emitted an organic genuineness that separated her. I couldn't analyze her because I didn't understand her. I was cynical—that much I knew about myself.

I had to spend some time with her but not get involved. I had to learn to break the cycle, to accept her without expectations. Maybe that's why she'd been put in my path.

I was justifying again. Damn!

* * *

It was a lazy Tuesday afternoon. First of the week business had been resolved and the books hadn't filled for mid-week yet, so I was in the rare position of having little to do. *Or had I set it up that way subconsciously?*

How was it then that with all my new-found good intentions, I wound up parking across the street from Blaze, like some kind of cop in a stake-out? How did I *not* look conspicuous? Sunglasses and lowered windshield visors and all? I was *looking* to get caught. It was the only believable rationale. I told myself I was using behavioral therapy. Be close enough to see her, watch her, but only from a distance. I could go through my cycle as normal, except I'd keep her out of reach. She wouldn't get hurt. It was an excellent plan. *Then why was I climbing out of my car and crossing the street to follow her into that restaurant?*

"Hello there."

She looked up from her salad, a fashion magazine spread open on the table in front of her. "You."

"Oh, so you remember me?"

She closed the magazine and motioned to the chair opposite her with a fork. "You may as well sit down since you're going to such trouble to follow me." Her voice was matter-of-fact.

"I... well, okay. Let me grab a sandwich and I'll join

you." I signaled a waiter and ordered a Reuben and a cup of coffee.

"That's an odd combination," she observed.

"Really? Why?"

"Well, I guess most people would order something cold and cleansing, like tea, to counter the spiciness of the corned beef and sauerkraut."

"Would they, now? You study people, do you? Or are you just trying to impress me?"

She looked down to her salad sheepishly and a thick lock of her hair dropped forward. She pushed it behind her ear in a habitual gesture I guessed she did a hundred times each day. I felt bad for snapping at her—she was probably caught off guard and said the first thing that came to mind. After all, I *had* ambushed her. I wondered why people chose hairstyles that needed tucking, straightening, pushing out of the eyes and so forth. Why not cut it or secure it with pins? It just seemed so... inefficient. *Oh, that's good. You're already getting to the critical part of the cycle. Heck, I might have her out of my system by bedtime. Yeah, right.*

"Yes, always have."

I'd been so deep in my introspection that I lost the thread of our conversation. I covered quickly.

"Why is that?"

She took another bite and tucked that strand behind her ear. "Not sure, really. I think maybe because I've always liked people, so I pay attention to what they say and do—you know a sort of respect thing."

She knew I'd been daydreaming. She could see right through me!

"May I ask you something?" She was looking at me directly and I could see she was focused on my eyes. I knew they were unusual and wasn't surprised. I was often complimented on them. I nodded to her to ask.

"Are you really so cocky and self-important that you think you can invade my life when I've clearly asked you to leave me alone?"

It was like someone had thrown a bucket of ice in my face. I wasn't used to being treated that way. When you grow up with money, people tend to try flattery and other means of getting in your good graces. Insults had never sat well with me. Why was I tolerating those from her? "Well, I might ask *you* something." Her eyebrows rose waiting for me to continue. "Are you always this rude to people who would like to get to know you?"

She stopped chewing and stared at me. "You know what? You're absolutely right. That wasn't the way I was raised. I apologize. How were you raised?"

I knew what she was getting at, and she knew that I knew. It was a rhetorical question and it put both of us in our proper places. Maybe there was some hope yet. I've never had to work this hard to get a girl before. I realized then, I was enjoying the process. It fell under that adage that said anything worth having was worth fighting for.

"So, can we start fresh? Can you forget that I was the evil, privileged one and simply see that someone was trying to take advantage of me?"

"Two more points. Looking back, I spent more time looking at you than I did at him. I didn't take the time to read him."

I liked what she said, even if it put me in a bad light. "You know, there just might be more to me than you think you see."

"But what if it's not all good?"

"But what if it's not all bad?"

She grinned, and I could tell she was intrigued by the thought of peeking inside the treasure chest. Except, that treasure chest was me. I wanted to be what would make her dreams come true. *Did I just say that?* Well, at least not aloud.

"I tell you what. Give it some time. I might grow on you."

"Should I get my shots first?"

This one was going to be a challenge. I took one last bite of my sandwich and threw a fifty on the table, wiping my mouth and signaling the waiter by putting my napkin over my plate. He'd spotted the fifty and couldn't get there fast enough. I pointed to her salad as well as my plate and waved my hand. "Keep the change," I told him. "And as for you, my young rebel, I only ask that you put away your hasty opinion of me. Who knows, you might start to like me." With that, I gave her a short salute and left the restaurant, my heart hammering in my chest. I didn't want to admit it, but she'd gotten to me. I needed some time to think it all over.

Chapter 6

Gwen

I couldn't even focus on my customers that afternoon. He'd gotten under my skin in a way that I had not let anyone do, at least not since Paul. I'd sworn to myself that I would always be my own woman; that I would never allow one shred of myself to be used by a man again. I was used to men coming on to me, I guess it was that tall blonde look that they love so well. Their eyes never went any deeper than my skin, though. That's the part I resented.

They didn't see the ambition and the love I was willing to give. They didn't see that I was a good mother to Carrie or the heartbreak imprinted by Paul. I didn't want to believe that all men could be that shallow. I'd always known men to be solution oriented. Couldn't they see that it was a better investment to get to know a girl first? Wasn't it worth their time to find a partner in life rather than a one-night stand in their bed? It was starting to look that way, but I hoped I was wrong.

When I thought about it, I could see I was being a little hypocritical. My job depended on women trying to please men, looking their best and making the men desire them. Were women nothing more than spiders, laying the web and waiting? There had to be more to it than that. Or maybe not? I knew I'd grown cynical since Paul. The little idealistic virgin had grown a thick skin and a bitter taste. It was possible that would mean I would be alone for the rest of my life, except for Carrie and whatever extraneous family members survived. Was that enough for me? I knew it wasn't. I wanted more than one child, I wanted a husband who loved and valued me. Most of all, I wanted redemption from the feeling that I'd been used and discarded. I knew that was what was bugging me. It wasn't fair for me to take out my resentment on every male who crossed my path.

I got home that evening to find Bitsy not even dressed for work. "What's up?"

"Oh, I took the night off."

"Are you feeling okay?" She looked away and didn't answer immediately. I could tell something was up. The question was, what was it?

"Yeah, I'm fine," she said slowly, filing her nails. The polish and topcoat waited patiently on the table next to her. I could see she'd chosen bright red and I knew something was up. That was the color she saved for special occasions.

I pulled Carrie out of the carrier, kissed her sweet face and took her to sit on my lap at the end of the sofa. I tickled her and loved the sound of her giggles. "So? Do I have to wait or are you going to tell me what's going on?"

"How do you do that?"

"What do you mean? How do I do what?"

"You know... You always know something is going on before anyone has to tell you. How do you read people like that?"

I shrugged. "I guess I just like people." I snapped my mouth shut, remembering my earlier introspection. How could I say I like people when I spent a good deal of time avoiding one entire half of them? "So? Spill it," I nudged her.

With an exasperated sigh she let her hands drop into her lap. "Okay, so, there's this party."

"Go on..."

"Well, I was sort of hoping you'd go with me."

She wasn't looking at me directly. Something was up. "Our usual crowd? Who's hosting it or are we going to another club?"

"Does that mean you'll go?"

Bitsy wasn't bright enough to realize I could see her traps coming. She thought she already had me committed but I was still picking her brain. "I didn't say that. In fact," I kicked off my shoes before continuing, "I've had a really lousy day and it would feel good just veg out and play with

Carrie."

Her bottom lip twisted, making her resemble a child who wasn't getting their way. "Why do you have to be so, so boring sometimes?"

I raised my eyebrows and looked at her. "Excuse me? Boring?"

She sighed, thinking for a moment to try a new track. "Okay, so as a 911 operator, my nights are never boring. Wouldn't you like, just occasionally, to live a little?"

"Why do I have the feeling you're trying to talk me into something I ordinarily wouldn't touch?"

Her eyes flared, and I could tell she knew she'd caught herself. She resumed filing her nails, holding her hand out to compare the arch on each finger. "I'm not. I just know that you work hard, and you never get out and I feel bad for you. I got invited to this party tonight and no, it's not our usual crowd. In fact, there might not be very many people we know it all. I thought maybe it would be a new experience and you'd like to go with me. Is there something wrong with that?"

She was trying to lead me down the trail of breadcrumbs. I wasn't going to give in that easily. I ignored her last question and went for the heart of the matter. "Whose party is it?"

"Does that matter?"

"To me it does."

"It's just sort of an open house. Well, an open condo."

"What is an open condo?"

"Funny you should ask. Why don't you go along with me tonight you'll find out?"

"Since when do we know someone who lives in a condo?"

"Look Gwen," Bitsy said with frustration. "Could you for just once go with me without asking a lot of questions? I already asked Mrs. Heathrow to watch Carrie and she has no problem. Just run in and grab a shower, I already took mine. Put on something pretty and let's just go. No questions asked. Can you do that for me?"

"Is this really important to you?"

"It really is."

"Then make up the diaper bag and I'm headed for the shower."

"I'm calling an Uber in case we want to have a little to drink tonight," Bitsy said as we handed Carrie over to Mrs. Heathrow. "It should be here any second." Her timing was perfect as we heard the horn honk out front.

"You be a good girl, Carrie," I told my daughter, kissing her on the head. "Now don't spoil her, Mrs. Heathrow. You make it hard for me to top you." Mrs. Hawthorne laughed and waved us goodbye as she closed the door behind me.

The Uber dropped us off on a corner and Bitsy was pulling my hand across the street toward an ultramodern building with balconies lighted like so many small stages. "Who lives here?"

"A friend of mine, never mind. You won't know anyone there so they'll all be new to you."

"I don't have a good feeling about this, Bitsy," I told her. "What floor is it on? Why don't you go on up ahead and give me a few minutes for some fresh air? My nerves are in a bundle and it's making me feel a little icky." She looked over her shoulder, but I couldn't read her expression.

"Okay," she agreed. "But you promise that you'll come up? You won't just call another car and go home?"

I nodded. "I promise."

Bitsy nodded, adjusted the waist on her mini pencil skirt and hurried toward the building. There were others coming and going, none of whom I recognized. There was a raised flower bed with a wide stone wall and I found a flat place where I could sit down and relax for a minute. I watched the people coming and going — all of them dressed in clothing I could've sold them from Blaze. Very upper class, very expensive, very beautiful people. It struck me that I didn't belong there and certainly Bitsy was out of place. These weren't her people, as much as they weren't mine. Nevertheless, a promise was a promise, so I took a deep breath and followed the current of bodies going inside.

Once inside the glass revolving doors, I was faced with a bank of elevators. Three doors opened at once and the others in the lobby crowded into two of them. The third one was still empty, so I took my cue and climbed aboard. The door shut, and I tapped the number 22 as Bitsy said that was our floor. I leaned against the back wall, crossing my legs at my ankles and held my clutch in front of me. I'd only gone three floors when the elevator came to a stop, and the doors opened. I was focused on my ankles and didn't look up and it wasn't until the door closed and I heard his voice that I knew who it was.

"Well, hello there," Colt greeted me.

"What are you doing here?"

He laughed aloud. "I might ask you the same thing. I happen to live here."

I knew my face flushed and I looked back to the floor

in embarrassment. "Bitsy is upstairs at a party, waiting for me." I hoped that was enough explanation.

"Which floor are you headed to?"

"22."

"Well, what you know? It would seem that you and I are going to the same party."

I looked up in shock. "Whose party is it?"

"Do you remember meeting Buddy at the club that night?" His blue eyes stared through mine as though I could hold no secrets from them.

I nodded.

"Well, he lives on the 22nd floor, and as you know I live on the fourth. I never was one for heights," he confided in me.

I didn't know what to say and wondered how it was that Bitsy came to be invited to Buddy's condo. I didn't have long to wonder as there was a jerk as the elevator came to a sudden stop.

"Hmmm," Colt said, pressing buttons on the panel to make the carrier move. It didn't budge. He tried the button to force open the doors, but it ignored him. He looked upward over our heads at the emergency panel. "We could always get out that way if we had to, but it would be safer if we waited here until someone comes to help." With that, he picked up the telephone inside the paneled access and when someone must've answered, he quickly told them our predicament. He hung up the phone and looked at me. "Some sort of a simple power failure, nothing dangerous. That's why the buttons aren't working, no power. I guess even the standby isn't coming on. So, just relax, they'll have us out of here no time."

As soon as he finished his words, the lights went out in the elevator and the two of us were alone in the darkness. I know I must have screamed a little because I felt his warm hand reaching out onto my arm. "Hey, it's okay. We're going to be just fine. It's just a power failure. Look, it's kind of weird standing up in the dark waiting for this thing to start moving. Let's sit down and make the best of it, shall we?"

I nodded.

"Shall we?" That's when I realized he didn't see me in the darkness. "Okay," I allowed, and he helped me slowly slide down the wall of the elevator until I was seated on the floor. Even though it was dark, I straightened my skirt, knowing the lights would eventually come back on and I didn't want it wrapped around my waist.

"Well, let's talk. It'll take our mind off things and before you know it, we'll be mobile again."

"Okay. What do you want to talk about?"

"Well, why don't you tell me about yourself? Where you grew up, about your family, your favorite color and maybe what you find sexy in a man?"

That last part caused me to suck my breath in. "Why do I feel like the last part of that question is the only thing you really wanted to know?"

"Not true. I'd like to know everything about you."

"I could say the same, you know? The enigmatic Mr. Stillman... The city's most eligible bachelor and the businessman extraordinaire."

"Do I hear a tone of disdain in your voice?"

"I'm sorry, I guess you do. I keep forgetting that I don't not like you."

"That you *don't not like me*? What does that mean?"

"I know, I'm all screwed up. I'm sorry, but it was just that you left such an impression on me in that courtroom that it's hard to feel anything but aggravation when I think about you."

His hand touched my arm and he began stroking the back of my hand. I had to admit it felt very comforting, warm and a little seductive. I could feel myself responding.

"Do you think it's just possible that you got the wrong impression?"

"This sounds like a conversation we had in the restaurant," I commented.

"I agree. Why don't we change the subject? Tell me about growing up. Where, who was your best friend, what you liked, what were you good at?"

His questions brought back a rush of old memories, all of which were shadowed by Paul and his abandonment. I still found it painful to talk about and even in the darkness, I didn't want tears in my eyes. As hard as I tried, it didn't work, though. I could feel them welling up, but I kept my hand on the floor as he stroked it. "Oh, not a very interesting past. I grew up in a small town, I had good parents and a lot of friends in school. I suppose you could call me a little popular, but then people always said that about cheerleaders."

"You were a cheerleader?"

"I loved it. I know it sounds trite, but when you're cheering for someone, you're always happy. Have you thought about that before? You can't cheer someone on and be angry at the same time."

He cleared his throat, a sound I found sexy as it came so close to my ear. When I sat very still I could even feel the ripples of his breath against my cheat. I wondered just how close he was but didn't have the guts to reach up with my other hand and find out. "Not being a cheerleader, I'll have to take your word for it. But, you strike me as an exceptional lady. I've thought so from the first moment I saw you."

I cocked my head a little at the thought. "Really? I had the idea that you would instantly hate everyone in the jury. I mean, isn't that the way it's supposed to be?"

"No, I don't think so. After all, when you know you're innocent you expect that the jurors will see that, and you'll soon be going home with the whole mess put behind you. It never occurred to me that anything else would happen."

"Huh, I never thought of it that way. Maybe that's why you looked to me to be so arrogant and self-assured. Maybe what I was seeing was competence of innocence?"

"There you go. Now you're getting warmer."

"I guess I was a little bit of a jerk to you, wasn't I?"

"No, not at all. I would expect if I were a juror that I would imagine the person to be guilty until he proved himself innocent, contrary to the orders they give you."

"You know? It was sort of like that. You figure the lawyers must have a pretty good case against the guy or woman if it went as far as a jury trial." Even in the darkness,

Colt was opening beams of light in my brain. I could feel his breath closer now and it smelled of brandy and a very masculine aftershave. I felt a single chill traveled down my spine and tried to set it aside. I couldn't afford to let myself be attracted to anyone, not as long as I had Carrie.

The elevator did a sudden little stutter stop, and then didn't move again. The lights were still off. I know I called out in fear and Colt slid his arm around me. I didn't resist. If we were going to fall to our death, at least I wouldn't be alone, although for the life of me I couldn't figure out why that made it any easier. I was illogical like that. His hand was stroking my upper arm as he pulled me against his chest. Again, I didn't resist. I hadn't been held by a man like that for a very long time and I liked it. Somehow it was easier in the dark, but I still liked it.

"Are you okay?" he whispered into my ear. He pulled me harder against him and his right hand moved up to the nape of my neck. His strong fingers began massaging the tense muscles in my shoulders dropped as they relaxed. There was another stutter stop and I pressed into him. His left hand came up and laid against my cheek, his thumb stroking my temple. "It's okay, Gwennie," he called me by my nickname. Oddly enough, I liked the sound of it. He drew in his breath then and that's when I felt his lips searching for mine. They were full and strong, pulling at mine until I allowed his tongue to open my mouth and sample my own. Without realizing it, I turned to face him and with the sort of surprised, but pleased intake of breath, he brought both arms around me and pulled me flat against him. He continued to kiss me, one hand riding up the back of my neck into the base of my hair, his long fingers pulling through the strands over and over. It was a seductive, sensitive touch and I understood intuitively that he probably knew my body better than his own. I shuddered, and he took it for fear although it was generated by pure lust. I even surprised myself.

He whispered something, but I couldn't catch what he said. It was drowned out in the sound of the elevator kicking back into motion. The lights flashed on and I quickly glanced downward to see that I had somehow managed to plaster myself against him, my legs spread open as I straddled his thighs. I blushed, and he smiled. "It's okay, it's just us," he said as he pushed to a stand and helped me up. There was just enough time for me to straighten my skirt before the elevator doors opened and the party burst in on us.

Bitsy was standing there, tapping her foot. "Where have you been? Why did you stop the elevator?"

"I didn't. The power went out and it stopped on its own. We've been trapped in the dark."

Bitsy's head spun around to look for someone and I wasn't the least bit surprised to see it was Buddy. He had a wicked grin on his face and suddenly I realized that we'd been the target of the conspiracy. I couldn't figure out why Bitsy was willing to take part in it, but when Buddy came closer and put his arm around her waist, I understood. I looked at Colt, but he was looking at me. I could tell he hadn't been in on it. That made me feel better, for some reason.

Colt came toward me, taking my hand and bent down to whisper in my ear. "I think we've been had. What do you say let's get out of here and go have a bite to eat?"

I took one look at Bitsy and Buddy and then nodded at Colt and followed him silently as he pulled me back into the elevator and slammed his hand on the button. "It was Buddy, wasn't it?" I asked quietly.

His back was to me. "I'd say that's a safe bet."

"You're angry, aren't you?"

He said nothing, but I pressed it.

"I'm sorry."

He turned on his heel and faced me. "No, you don't understand. It has nothing to do with you, in fact I could be trapped in the space shuttle with you for a year and not mind it." His words took my breath away, but he wasn't finished. "It's Buddy. He works for me, not the other way around. I don't like him taking things in his own hands. It's just a control thing I have. I have a tough time trusting people, but I'm sure you don't understand that. Everyone must love you, you're so good and cheerful."

"You may be surprised," I muttered, thinking of Paul and the trust I'd lost. "Look, I think this was Bitsy's doing. She's kind of wacky like that, getting involved where she shouldn't. She's an emergency operator and to her it's instinct to help people. Even if they don't want her help. I wouldn't blame this on Buddy. I have a feeling it was her idea and he probably went along with it to score some points. Let's just drop it?"

He gradually burst into a grin. "Agreed."

"Did you drive?" Colt asked me as we exited the building.

"Bitsy and I came in an Uber, in case we both had too much to drink."

"Excellent, my driver will be here in a moment."

"You have a driver?"

"Well, didn't you?"

"Oh, I guess so, but it's not exactly the same. At least I'm betting it's not," I answered and had no more than finished my sentence before a dark charcoal limousine with heavily tinted windows pulled up to the curb. "I guess I was right."

"Would you feel better if I called us an Uber?"

"This is just new for me, I'm sorry."

"Don't be sorry. Just relax and enjoy it."

I knew his words were intended to set me to ease, but he had no idea the memories it conjured.

A text popped up on my phone. It was from Bitsy. "**Saw you leave. I've got Carrie for the night, don't hurry home.**"

I responded. "**You set me up, Miss Judas. But, it's not like that, only going to dinner.**"

"**Uh, huh. Just in case, your bases are covered.**"

"You ready? Everything okay?" Colt asked.

I nodded as the driver opened the door and I climbed into the next part of my life.

Chapter 7

Coulter

I felt excitement in my gut at the idea of having Gwen all to myself for at least a couple of hours. Every conversation we had was stimulating—she presented a challenge to me. She reminded me of a doe; dewy-eyed innocence coupled with a quivering defense that promised she would bolt at the first inclination. There was something about her that made me want to protect her, to shield her from whatever it was that had her so frightened. I knew she was hiding something; she had to be. Only people with secrets didn't want to talk about their past. What could be so horrendous in her short life?

I took her to Barney's—a restaurant and bar known among people with money who wanted excellent food and even greater discretion. We were both a little under-dressed, but I was well-known there, and they'd never risk my future business or referrals by turning me down at the door. Or so I hoped.

The maître d' recognized me and came around from his podium to speak to me privately. "Sir, as you know there is a jacket policy. I will be happy to show you and your guest to one of our private alcoves if you wouldn't mind wearing a jacket on loan as you pass through the dining room?"

I nodded and smiled, marveling at how they handled such old-fashioned policies. It was how old money behaved; clinging with their last dollars' worth of grip to a time that was more traditional and held in check by social rules than the present. He promptly removed a jacket from the coat rack, holding it up so that I might slide it on. He looked briefly at Gwen but decided he had pushed it enough. “If you'll follow me?” he asked and took us to one of the single table, private dining alcoves at the far end of the restaurant. These could only be offered, they could not be requested. We both stood aside as Gwen entered and stood next to the table, a question in her eyes. I quickly slid off the jacket and threw it over the back of an extra chair, circling around to pull her chair out for.

“I think I'm a little underdressed,” she commented.

“You weren't planning on coming here, obviously, but it's okay. They know me here.”

“So, I figured out.”

The maître d' fussed around us, opening the door to admit a waiter with a bucket of champagne and two crystal flutes. He handed us menus, but Gwen shook her head. “You order for me.”

“No problem.” I knew what was bothering her; the menu was in French and had no prices. I didn't want her to be embarrassed. “Thank you for letting me,” I said, patting the back of her hand. "I have some favorites here and I'd like to introduce you to them."

Finally, we were alone and the candle on the table between us flickered invitingly. I would have preferred her at my condo where we were truly alone. "Can I ask you something?"

She nodded. "Yes..."

"You don't have to answer if you don't want to. I'll understand."

"Go ahead."

"I get the feeling that you're hiding some kind of secret."

Her head snapped up and I was drawn to the long, lovely line of her throat. I could almost taste that sweet flesh and the heat in my groin echoed the desire. "What makes you say that?" There was alarm in her eyes, which only convinced me I was on the right track.

I reached across the table, running my index finger across the back of her hand. She jumped, and I caught her before she pulled it back. I moved the finger, stroking the inside of her palm. "You know... there is some truth to the saying that trusting someone is the greatest gift you can give them."

She didn't say a word, another clue that she was hiding something and not willing to divulge it. I decided to give up on it for the time being. I wanted her to trust me.

"So, tell me about your work," she prodded, changing the subject.

"Not as exciting as you might think. Just a bunch of concrete, steel, and glass." I didn't like to talk about my company—it had long before lost its appeal and challenge. I would have liked to have sold out the whole thing, but until I found something I liked better, it kept me busy.

Food and drink were ferried to and from the room and I could tell that Gwen was beginning to loosen up. I made a few corny jokes and she laughed as though I was the most brilliant comedian she'd ever heard. I shared some stories from when I was young and in boarding school. She listened, wide-eyed and never interrupted. Her silence became conspicuous. "Sorry, I'm boring you," I said, pushing my chair back and relaxing with a goblet of after dinner wine.

Her head shook before she found her voice. It was sleepy, and she slurred a bit—not in a sloppy way, but in the most cuddly, endearing way. "You're not boring, not even a little," she purred. "It's just that I've never known anyone like you."

"Not like me in what way?"

She pulled back her head like a chicken getting ready to cluck and I could tell that she was wobbly. "Let's just say people like you didn't grow up down the street from me. You had, well... you had everything."

I shook my head. "It's not that simple. Sure, we didn't worry about the electric bill, but my parents still fought, and I was shy in school. I caught the flu, skinned my knees, and my dad made me work for my spending money. It wasn't all that different," I told her.

She was already shaking her head again. "It might look like that from your side, but not from mine. You haven't walked in my shoes." She snapped upright then as if she'd said too much. I read it in her eyes. Then, at least I knew the source of whatever she was hiding.

I texted my driver and stood up, pulling on the jacket before I circled the table and helped her stand up. Her legs were wobbly and she leaned into me. Her body felt so good against mine. We walked slowly through the dining room and I slid off the jacket and laid it on the podium as we went out the door and into the limo.

Gwen was soft and warm against me on the car's seat. Her breath was slightly fruity from the wine and her hair shone in the streetlights as we sped beneath them. She didn't ask where we were going, and I didn't bring it up. It would make sense that I'd take her back to the building where both Buddy and I lived.

We pulled up to the revolving door and the granite building was iconic against the skyline. I had to admit it was impressive and that was one of the reasons I'd chosen to move there. When I moved in, Buddy got a bad case of one-upmanship and bought a condo as well, although on a higher floor. He could keep the height.

Gwen was silent as I unlocked my door and a motion detector triggered a few ceiling canisters dimmed low. The liquor had really gotten to her and I realized she probably wasn't used to drinking. I wouldn't take advantage of her, but oh, God, how easy it would have been.

She stumbled, and I caught her, scooping her into my arms as I carried her back to the guest room next to the master. She was sleepy and didn't offer an argument. I managed to pull back the coverlet and lay her on the bed before removing her shoes and lifting her legs to the mattress. A shaft of moonlight fell over her in the darkened room, making her features soft and mysterious. She was watching me, and I knew instinctively that I was being judged. This was where the trust would be built.

I sat on the edge of the mattress, lifting a strand of her long hair and letting it cascade through my fingers. "You going to be okay? There's a bath right there at the foot of the bed if you feel sick or anything. Want me to get you a washcloth?"

"No, I'm okay," she whispered, her huge eyes searching my face warily. "Where are you going to sleep?"

I jerked my head in the direction of the master. "Just on the other side of that wall is my room. I'll leave the door open in case you need something. Hey, let me grab a shirt or something you can sleep in," I told her and got up. When I came back, I held out a navy t-shirt I wore around the house. It had been washed enough times that it was soft and although she might drown in it, at least she could move better than that tight skirt she was wearing. "Can you change yourself?"

Gwen's eyes grew huge and she nodded, holding up her hand to brush me away. "I'm okay," she mumbled sleepily again, and I bent over and kissed her cheek, just as if she was a young child being tucked into bed. She looked very innocent just then and my body was reacting. I needed to leave.

"Okay, well, goodnight then," I whispered and got up, giving her one last look before I left the room. "Remember, I'm right next door. Just call out if you need something."

It felt like trying to pull away from a magnet. I forced myself to go into my room and turn on the nightstand lamp. I took a quick, coolish shower to diminish the throbbing need she instilled in me and pulled back the crisp sheets to climb beneath. A housekeeper came every day to clean and prepare my meals. She was meticulous in her cleanliness and the sheets were changed daily. They were crisp and felt good against my bare skin. I kept trying to keep myself in the moment. When I let myself become distracted, all I could think of was Gwen lying on the other side of the wall alone, and how vulnerable she'd looked. I knew I wouldn't get much sleep and turned on the nightstand Echo and let it play the sound of distant thunderstorms. I found it soothing, but still, it spoke to the primitive inside me and with each roll of thunder, I could feel my need for Gwen growing.

My back was to the door when I felt a subtle movement of the bed. A waft of cool air swept over my legs as Gwen's body slid beneath the covers. She scooted toward me and I felt the soft cotton of the t-shirt against my back. "Would you mind terribly if I slept in here with you? I know it's silly, but I get a little spooked when I'm in strange places."

I rolled over and slid my arm beneath her. "Sure, you can. I get a little spooked myself sometimes when I'm traveling and in a strange hotel," I murmured as I pulled her against me and she curled like a young girl to conform to the shape of my hip. But there was nothing but woman beneath that cotton shirt. I began to stroke her upper arm and with every pass of my hand I could feel the muscles beneath her skin relax and conform to me. "Gwen, answer something for me?" I asked softly.

"Hmm...?" she responded in a voice as thick as honey.

"Who am I and where are we?"

I heard her breath pause momentarily before she answered. "Colt Stillman and I'm pretty sure this is where you live."

"Good girl," I exhaled as I rolled onto my hip and pulled her to face me. Her face turned upward, and I met her lips with a hard kiss; it was filled with the residue of frustration and need for the woman in my arms. Her lips answered mine, parting so I could taste her tongue and the sweet moisture of her inside cheek. Then began the give and take of lovers—the quest from one followed by the answer of the other. Gwen was tentative and tender. I recognized immediately she'd had few lovers in her life. I suspected one had hurt her and that was what she could not, or would not, share. I swore I would drive his memory from her. Whatever he'd done had left pain and I would take it away and replace it with the tenderness and protection a woman like her deserved to feel from a man.

Even that aside—I wanted her. I wanted her more than any woman I'd ever known. She wasn't just a body; she was a simple and yet intensively complicated vessel holding all a man could ever need or want. She was meant for me. She just didn't know it yet because she was too scared to open herself. I would change all that.

Kissing her, I moved my fingertips to her nipples, taking each in turn and rubbing them gently in circular motions through the fabric. They responded to my touch, becoming erect and I felt the breath in her throat quicken. With one, smooth motion, I pulled the shirt over her head, pulling her nipples into my mouth. Gwen began squirming, her hips driving into the mattress as her body arched, lifting her breasts against my face. I fed upon her and then loosed one hand to push her panties down the long extension of her legs. She opened herself to my touch and as I suckled, I pressed against her woman's grotto with my finger.

Her reaction was organic and naturally female. She pumped her hips, trying to seat my finger more deeply. I was gentle but decided as I rose above her and entered her. Gwen bucked upward and with a steady, but firm movement, I pushed her back down against the bed. Slowly and with caution I penetrated her depth and then slid out, giving her a split second's respite before I moved into her once again. Over and over we repeated the dance of mankind, growing in intensity until we crested the peak and the shudders washed over us.

As thoughts cleared, I clutched her against me, my hand cupping that which I'd just breached—she belonged to me then and I would protect her from that moment on.

Chapter 8

Gwen

A strange light was seeping through my eyelids the next morning. I lay very still, aware that my surroundings were unfamiliar and wondering what time it was. I panicked a little when I realized that I didn't hear Carrie breathing in her crib and that's when it all came back. I felt the bed move and lifted one eyelid just enough to sneak a glance. Colt's back was to me as he was seated on the edge of the bed, running his hand through his hair and stretching. I quickly pulled my eyes shut until I felt him stand and then I heard a door shut. There was water running and I recognized he was in the shower. Without hesitating another moment, I slid from the bed, rescued my panties and stole down the hall to the bedroom where I'd started. Pulling on my clothes, I ran toward his door. I managed to open and shut it quietly closed behind me, and then I was pulling on shoes in the elevator. I only had moments to pull myself together, whipping a comb out of the bottom of my purse. Then I was at street level and the revolving door deposited me on the sidewalk. I walked, no, it was more like ran, to the corner, fishing out my phone. I called Uber and told them where I was. I told them to look for me to be walking west on Guillemot Avenue, and they should come and pick me up. The driver must not have been far away because it wasn't very long before there was a horn beeping behind me. I jumped into the backseat and in a matter of a few miles, I was home.

It was very early and Bitsy was still asleep, as was Carrie, safely in her crib. I wanted to pick her up so badly but didn't want to disturb her. I pulled fresh clothing out of the drawer and went into the bathroom to shower. I could hear Carrie, her little voice tweeting like a bird when I emerged. I warmed a bottle and climbed onto my bed, the covers still made from the night before and held her in my lap as I fed her. That was when the guilt really began to sink in.

I'd let it happen again. I'd sworn to myself I would never be someone's one-night stand, not ever again. And yet all it took were a few glasses of wine and one helluva handsome stud to convince me otherwise. I felt confused and lonely at the same time. Carrie's brown eyes looked up at me, trusting me and I knew I'd let her down, too. When she was done eating I rocked her against my chest, humming a lullaby when Bitsy appeared in the doorway.

"What time did you get in?"

"A while ago."

I could see her choosing her words carefully. "Did you have a good time?"

I shrugged but didn't say anything and I think she knew she wasn't going to get anything further out of me. She turned and went into the kitchenette and made us each a cup of coffee. I joined her on the sofa and we watched the news, played with Carrie between us and didn't talk about the night before. My cell phone began ringing in the other room and Bitsy looked at me sideways when she realized I wasn't getting up to answer it. She was smart enough not to say anything. I pretended I heard nothing. We spent the late morning and early afternoon washing up some laundry; an old movie with Barbara Stanwick played on the screen as we folded clothes between us. It was one of those morning-after kind of days when you hadn't gotten enough sleep but had too much to drink and was still feeling it.

My cell rang twice more, and I continued to ignore it. At one point, I picked up a stack of clothes and went into the room to put them away, switching the phone to silent. That was one way to deal with it.

Sometime in the later afternoon, I took Carrie to bed with me and we both had a nap. I found a book to read and stayed in my room, while Carrie played with toys in her crib. It was a very domestic and tranquil evening, but somehow it was still lonely. My phone continued to ring.

The next morning it was back to normal. I dressed and went to work, trying not to think about what I'd done. I felt overwhelmed with guilt and disappointment in myself. I knew that Colt would never think of me in a serious light—he was under no obligation. He was used to getting what he wanted, wealthy men were like that. Not to mention he was extremely well-connected and powerful in business. I was a toy he pursued because I was elusive and once he had me, that would be the end. I never even checked my phone to see who'd been calling; just covered the names and numbers as I systematically tapped the trashcan.

I was off my game and one of the other clerks asked me if something was wrong. I muttered something quietly and unintelligible and she seemed to get the message. At lunchtime, I left through the back door and went somewhere I'd never been before. I was afraid he was tracking me again and as he had before, he could've ended up at my lunch table with me. I didn't want to see him. I had to forget Colt Stillman. He was just another checkmark in the column already populated by Paul.

I was uncomfortable all afternoon. I felt as though people could read my face and knew what I'd done. I knew things were different in a bigger city—that I was still thinking like a small-town cheerleader. But that's who I was inside. By that evening, I've made up my mind. I told Bitsy I was going to spend a quiet evening in with Carrie. She was getting dressed to go to work.

"Have you answered his calls yet?" she finally asked.

"What you mean?"

"Don't be coy," she muttered, and I had to admit although it was a short word, I was surprised she understood it.

"He's not interested in me, Bitsy. Men like Colt don't hang onto women like me."

"What are you talking about? What do you mean by women like you? What's wrong with you?" Her eyes were wide and bugging out. I realized that she held me to a standard I didn't quite identify with.

"He can have anyone he wants." I was trying to change the subject.

"He wants you."

"You don't know that. You don't know anything about him. I barely know him, and I saw how he lives. His kind just uses people like me as toys. When they're broken, they throw them away."

"He's not like that, Gwen. He's been calling constantly. Why don't you answer the phone?"

"You don't know that, either. Look, you see that little girl there with her toys? That's what came from trusting a man. No man is going to complete me. They're not to be trusted, haven't you learned by now?"

Bitsy stepped around the doorway from the bathroom, her hairbrush in her hand. "No, to tell you the truth, I haven't. Maybe I've been lucky, and just maybe I haven't been cynical."

"It's a pretty big word for you," I said with spite. She was getting under my skin.

"Whatever. You do what you want to but leave me out of it. Colt is quite a catch and for you to dump him like that makes no sense. But then, most of the time, you don't make sense at all."

She said her peace, grabbed her purse and slammed the door behind her. Tears burned in my eyes. How had it come to this? Just two days earlier I was being pursued by the most eligible bachelor in town and had a best friend who I thought would have my back no matter what. Now I wasn't speaking to one and the other one wasn't speaking to me. What the hell happened?

I grabbed my cell and plopped down on the sofa, tapping Metallica's private cell number. I heard myself tell her that I had a family emergency and needed some time off. I asked that she hold my job if possible and she reassured me if I came back within three weeks, it would be mine. I thanked her and hung up. I doubted three weeks would be enough to get my life back in shape, but at least I kept that option open. With a sigh, I went into the bedroom and pulled my suitcases out from beneath the bed. I filled them with the simpler items of my wardrobe and all of Carrie's things. I tied things together with bungee cords, including her porta crib. The Uber was waiting for me by the time we got down to the street. An hour later we were on a

Greyhound, headed home to Brookfield. I wasn't sure my car was up to the trip and besides, I didn't want people to recognize me as I came into town. I'd left Bitsy a brief explanatory note saying I'd gone to see my parents.

The bus station was busy as we pulled into town. I saw familiar faces and a few hands raised in my direction. I could tell at least one of the girls was headed over to talk to me, but I quickly threw my things into the back of the taxi that was waiting beside the station and climbed in with Carrie in my lap. I knew it would soon be all over town that I had come home, and most of them would think it was in defeat. Small town people tended to be that way, always jealous of those who tried to make more of themselves and quietly rejoicing when they fail. I felt rotten about everything in general. The city had been my dream and now here I was back in this tiny little town looking for refuge with my parents. Talk about a step backward, I had just taken a giant one.

My parents were thrilled to see me but somewhat puzzled by what was going on. I couldn't blame them. I wasn't much more than a child myself and certainly didn't have a track record of making wise choices. They knew nothing about Colt and I wanted to keep it that way. I did my best to chatter on to Mom and Dad about all the wonderful things I'd seen in the city. I told them about my job and about Bitsy but left out anything that had to do with Colt Stillman. I talked about the world of high fashion and how elegant the salespeople were. Mom said she was proud of me and I think she was sincere. She didn't have a choice to be anything other than that.

We were just finishing up when the phone rang. Mom and Dad still had an old rotary landline, so I signaled with my hand that I would get it.

"Hello?" I spoke into the cradle and liked the way it fit in my hand. Cell phones were great, but these were more comfortable.

No one responded, but I could hear an engine running in the background. It might've been a car, but it was too far away to tell for sure.

"Hello?" I tried once more and when there was no response again, I hung up. Mom looked at me as I reentered the room, her eyebrows raised in question. "Wrong number, I guess." She was bringing in a tray with cups of coffee, including one for me.

"I thought you might be a coffee drinker by now?"

I laughed. As a matter of fact, you're right. Everybody drinks coffee, it's the center of social life if you don't count the bars and I never was much of a barfly."

"Oh, heavens, no," Mom muttered. "At least you haven't gone there."

That stung. They'd never said anything, but I knew they were disappointed in me. I'd always been a high achiever, top of my class, head cheerleader, you name it. That had ended after one night with Paul and although Mom and Dad loved Carrie dearly and would never trade her for my old reputation, I could tell just in that single remark that Mom had been holding her breath to see how low I would fall before I hit bottom.

I let it go. My parents' house was the only shelter I could count on at the moment. After my fight with Bitsy, I wasn't entirely sure she'd be waiting when I got back. I felt like everything in my life was on trial at the moment. The only person I could trust was my tiny daughter.

I tried to relax into the home atmosphere and sat quietly in a side chair holding Carrie as my parents watched their post-news game shows and whatever version of CSI was currently in vogue. I stared at the screen, feigning interest but my mind was swirling. I could feel Colt's mouth on mine and the gentle touching that caused my nipples to harden. I felt the heat low in my belly just from remembering... No! I wasn't allowed to remember that. I couldn't go through cataclysmic rejection—not again. Colt was not intended for me. He would marry the daughter of some wealthy politician or businessman... someone with the right background and connections to advance his business. Wealthy people didn't seem to have a limit to their desire for more and more money. They were playing games and money was the way they kept score. My face burned as I realized I might be one of those score marks, but I'd paid with my flesh and my heart. As much as I hated to admit it, I had developed feelings for Colt—even if they were only a sense of being protected.

I called it a night early; there was only so much network programming I could take. Mom and Dad gave Carrie goodnight kisses and cuddles and I got a pat on the shoulder. I wasn't their little girl any longer.

Upstairs, I switched on the overhead light in my old bedroom. The porta-crib was set up. I changed Carrie and laid her down. She was such a good child and gave me a sweet smile before she fixated on a mobile hung overhead and then slowly closed her eyelids and dropped off to sleep. I changed my clothes and folded back the covers. Snapping off the light switch, I traveled the well-remembered six steps to the side of my bed and sat down, pulling my brush from the nightstand. I always gave my long, thick hair a hundred strokes. It wasn't so much about grooming as it was the comforting ritual that was self-soothing. It was a time for reflection, although that night, it felt more like revisiting guilt.

Laying down the brush, I slid my feet beneath the sheets and puffed the pillow. Just as I was about to lie down, I heard a car approach our house at a high speed, brake out front, and then peel off with tires spinning. I rolled to my knees to look out the window but all that was left was a pair of taillights in the distance before they disappeared over a rise in the road. My heart pounding, I rolled back to lie down. I lay awake for a long time that night, wondering who had been driving. My gut told me that it was the man who was so very good at tracking me and appearing out of nowhere. It had to be Colt; he likely had my parents' address and had tracked me long enough to know I would be there. A short flight and a rental car later, he was watching my house and did it loudly enough to let me know he was there. What was it that made me shudder? Relief or fear?

Coming back to Brookfield was nice, but obviously, there was nowhere for me to hide from the inquisitive Mr. Stillman. I needed to settle things with him before I lost my job and gave up whatever security I'd build for Carrie and myself. I couldn't let him ruin the new life I'd built.

The next morning, I fibbed and told Mom I'd gotten a text from my boss and that someone had quit, and they needed me back pronto. "I can't afford to make them mad, Mom. I haven't had the job long and I really need to make a go of it."

She nodded, thoughtful. "To tell you the truth, I've been wondering why you came home at all. You couldn't have built up vacation this early. Did something happen there? Is something wrong?"

"No, just got homesick," I fibbed again, my mind saying *yes, something happened okay. He's tall with black hair, blue eyes and charisma dripping from his lips. I'm in trouble—real trouble.*

Carrie and I left the next morning.

Chapter 9

Coulter

What in the hell happened? One minute she's in bed next to me and the next, she vanished. She knew where she was and who she was with. What went wrong?

This string of questions raged through my brain like an overflowing river. I decided to give her a few days to calm down or come to her senses; depending on what applied. In the meantime, I had a business to run.

Mason Derry was sitting across the desk from me, a folder of papers in his hand and a puzzled look on his face. His reading glasses had slid down to the tip of his nose.

"I thought you were going to have this all sort out?" I yelled at him. "Every day those permits are withheld, I'm losing millions. So, here's what I'm going to do. Until you get this mess cleaned up, don't bother billing me because you're not cutting it!" My hands were literally quivering with my rage and at the same time, my stomach was rolling from nerves and the fifth of bourbon I'd put away the night before on the floor of my living room. Alone.

"Woah, Colt, calm down."

"Don't tell me to calm down. Don't sit there making

excuses or rolling this off on me. You're the one in the hot seat. You should have seen this kind of shit coming and sheltered the risk a long time ago. It took some moron loser of an ex-employee to cause this gargantuan, fucking mess? What the hell were you doing to protect my interests? Golfing? Fucking somebody's wife?" I was pounding my desk.

Mason closed his folder and took off the ridiculous glasses. "I can see we're not going to get anywhere here today. You want to fire me, then fire me. But you'll have a bigger mess on your hands than you do right now. I don't think you're one bit upset about the permits—you've been in this business far too long to get shook like this. There's something else going on, Colt, and it has nothing to do with me. Call me when you've calmed down," he finished and left my office. I threw an ink pen at the door as it closed behind him.

There was a tap on my door and it opened. Buddy's head poked around the side of it. "What the hell is going on in here?" he asked, although he was careful to keep his voice level and low.

"Just the person I was looking for. What have you got to do with this whole thing?"

"Excuse me?"

"Don't play innocent. I know you and that ditzy

girlfriend of hers teamed up to get us together and I no more got her past hating me and she's disappeared. What you know about this?"

Buddy came in and shut the door quietly, but firmly behind himself. He held out his hands. "Well, Colt, calm down now. I've never seen you like this before. You're letting a woman get to you?"

"She's not just any woman!" I shouted, throwing another pen at him. Lucky for me he was able to back away before I took out his eye.

"Damn! I've never seen you hot like this, not even in a fight."

"Fights are fair, this isn't."

Buddy sat down in the chair opposite my desk that Mason had just vacated. "Okay, let's talk about this," he said in a very calm voice. "First of all, she hasn't disappeared from the face of the planet. You can find her, you can always find anyone you want. I think you're aggravated because she doesn't want to find you. You're not used to being treated that way."

"You're sure as hell right about that," I muttered and swiveled my chair so I was staring out the window. "I feel like that line in the old Bogie movie. Of all the gin joints why did she have to walk into mine?"

"Look, Colt. Give her some space. I don't know a whole lot about her, but I do know that she's a good person. Bitsy thinks the world of her and as wacky as Bitsy might seem, she's got street smarts. She works with every crappy crime you can think of every day and she still manages to stay sane. I haven't talked to her about this and, frankly, I had no idea you were this upset. You're taking this way too personally."

"Oh, really? How would you take it if you were really into a lady and she came home with you but disappeared before you got out of the shower the next morning?"

Buddy winced. "Oh, yeah, that is bad. But only if you didn't want her to leave. I can think of a few times I wish they would've left as soon as the fun was over."

I slammed my fist on my desk. "She's not like that," I jabbed my finger at him. "You got that?"

"Got it, got it. Okay, here's what we're going to do. And for once you're going to take orders from me. I'm going to get up from this chair and I'm going back to my office. I'm going to give Bitsy a call and invite her to lunch. I'll find out what I can from her, but I don't know how much she knows. When I come back, I'll come in and talk to you and tell you what I've learned. But between then and now, you're going to go through your calendar and start setting up appointments. We've got one hell of a lot of guys standing around doing nothing, still on the payroll. We have buildings that must go up and we have permits to secure before we can do that. It's all on you at this point, Colt. There's only so much I can do on my own." He stood up and walked away from my desk, stopping as he was ready to open the door. "She really got to you, didn't she?" he said quietly over his shoulder.

"Yeah, she really got to me," I admitted.

* * *

Buddy was back a couple of hours later. He wasted no time. "She's been out of town, apparently went to see her parents. She's back but doesn't want to see you. I don't know why—don't know what happened, but that's it. Sorry, Colt." I could see the trepidation on his face as he unloaded the information. He was probably nervous that I'd go off on him again.

"Nothing more?"

"Nope," he shook his head.

"Okay. I'm taking the rest of the day off. Look after things, will you?" I didn't wait for a response but swept past him on my way out. I had my own ways of finding her—I'd already proven that.

* * *

"You."

The young woman at the reception desk looked up at me and practically fell off her stool. I didn't know her name. "Me?"

"Your name, please?"

"I'm Monica Stewart, Mr. Stillman." Her pretty face was furrowed with what almost looked like fear.

"Monica, come with me." I motioned and strode toward the exit that led to the garage. I turned around and she was sitting there with her mouth hanging open. "Are you coming?"

"Uh, yes, right behind you," she said, grabbing her purse from her drawer and stumbled to catch up. I held the door open for her and pointed to my car which was in my personal spot next to the door.

Unlocking it, I opened the door and motioned for her to get inside. She stood there, undecided and nervous. "It's okay. I need a young woman to go shopping for me and you look like you'll fit the bill."

I guess it was the magic word "shopping" but she instantly seemed more interested and cooperated by climbing in. On the ride over to Blaze, I expected what I wanted her to do.

"You are going to be like a secret shopper, but instead of checking out clothes, I want you to look for a certain young woman. Her name is Gwen and she's a tallish blonde but her most unusual feature is her huge turquoise eyes."

"Okay, but what do I say when I find her?"

"Oh, no, don't talk to her. Not unless you can't help it, and don't tell her I sent you. Here," I reached into my pocket and pulled out a gold card. "Buy yourself some clothes, I don't care what, but the reason you're there is to look for her, pay attention to how she's behaving and whether she looks happy. Can you do that?"

"Well, sure. That's not work at all."

I handed her the card. "Remember, this is not about shopping, this is about connecting with her state of mind."

"Got it," she snapped the card from my hand as we pulled up to the curb and she got out.

"I'll be across the street in that parking garage, bottom floor. Come find me. I'll be watching."

She nodded and almost tripped in her haste to get into the store. I hoped she could contain herself enough to get the information I wanted.

An hour later, she came back, trailing through the

parking garage with armloads of bags and a salesgirl trailing her with a luggage dolly piled with boxes strapped together. I got out of the car and loaded these in the trunk, avoiding a direct look at the salesgirl. I tipped her a hundred-dollar bill which she tucked it into her bra and then swung her hips broadly as she retreated.

We climbed into the car and I left the garage by the back exit. "So?"

Monica shifted in her seat, so she was facing me. "First, thank you for the clothes," she said, pulling the card out of her blouse and laying it on the console between us. "I know who you were looking for. She was there. Tall and leggy? Busty?"

I nodded. "That's her."

"She seemed quiet, but she was working side by side with a very tall African woman with to-die-for cheekbones. I think I heard her called Metallica."

"Okay, but what about Gwen?"

"She was really focused on what the Metallica woman was telling her. I got the idea that she was in training for something, like maybe a promotion. I tried to shop close by. I heard Metallica ask her if she intended to make Blaze her career or was she more interested in marriage and a family over the long term."

Monica paused. I had to ask. "What did she say."

She drew a breath, I think she knew I wasn't going to like the answer. "She said she never wanted to be married."

* * *

I dropped my car off back at the office and went to a bar not far from where Gwen worked. I knew what time she'd be off, and I'd be waiting. I ordered a double whiskey and settled back in a dark booth at the far side of the room from the door where I could watch. I was starting on my third when I looked down at my phone and saw it was close to her quitting time. I threw a hundred on the table and walked out into the sunlight, squinting a little and off tilt until I could adjust my eyes. Then I saw her; she was standing next to a very tall African woman. That was obviously the one that Monica had referenced. I hung back, watching, while the women chatted briefly on the sidewalk. Eventually, the Metallica lady turned and left and then Gwen turned in the opposite direction. She never heard me come up behind her until I grabbed her arm gently and she jumped.

"What?" flew from her mouth in surprise.

"Gwen, I have to talk to you."

"Well, I don't have to talk to you," she said cruelly,

pulling her arm away from me. She tried to turn and walk away but I wouldn't let her go. I caught up next to her and spoke as we headed toward her car.

"Gwen, please, stop." I tried to put my arms around her, but she pushed me away. I pulled her hard against my chest and trapped her, my hand holding the crown of her head. "Shhhh... now hold on here. I'm not your enemy. Hey, now stop a minute—you owe me that much."

"I owe you?" She was flushed and angry, but she did stop fighting me. The huge turquoise eyes looked up at me and welled up with tears. "What do you want from me?"

"Hey," I lowered my voice again, "let's just go across the street and have some wine and talk. What do you say?"

She shook her head. "No, I have to get home."

"You've got time. What's the rush?"

"I have to go, that's all," she said and pushed back, heading to a car parked at the curb. I assumed it was hers. She fiddled with the lock and then threw her things inside in frustration as I stood on the sidewalk, watching. I could see her jamming the key into the ignition, but the car didn't start. I heard the give-away click-click that suggested her battery was dead.

Walking around to the driver's window, I tapped, and

she cranked down the window. At least no power windows, I thought and then felt bad. “Gwen, come on out of there. I’ll drive you home and send a wrecker to pick up your car. I’ll get it sorted out for you and have it brought to your place when it’s fixed. C’mon now.”

I opened her door and she sat there, chewing her lip in deliberation.

"You really don't have a lot of other choices, you know," I told her. "I thought you said you were in a hurry?"

"She looked up at me. "I am, okay, okay. Drop me off at my apartment building, please?"

"No problem, come with me," I held up my hand and she slid out of the car and stood up, smoothing her skirt. The sight of her legs took my breath away, but I had to control myself if I was going to get to the bottom of whatever was bothering her. "I'm parked just down the street."

She nodded and followed me, holding my hand as I had offered. She was that kind of a woman. There were times when she was like a little girl and times when she was a willful, strong-minded and stubborn woman who would never allow herself to be taken advantage of. That revelation gave me pause for thought. I deposited her in my car and walked around to the driver’s side. I slid in and looked over, her skirt had slid up her thighs and it was all I could do to not reach over and touch her. I remembered what she felt like and how she smelled. She was all sweetness and innocence. I reined myself in and revved the engine, pulling out into traffic. "Want to give me directions?"

She looked at me sidelong. "You're kidding, right? You've known where I live from the very beginning. You wouldn't let a little thing like that escape your attention."

"No, I suppose I wouldn't." I let the subterfuge pass and wondered when she'd caught on to me. She was a very bright woman and that was part of the reason she held such an attraction for me.

"You can just let me out at the corner," Glenn said as she motioned to the upcoming street.

"No, you don't. We have some unsettled business between us. I think at the very least, you owe me an explanation of why you ran out on me. I didn't expect anything from you if you remember you came into my room."

"Do we have to go over all that now?" I could tell the topic upset her and I had to know why. It was that nagging feeling that somebody was lying to me, and that always raised the specter that I was about to be stabbed in the back. I couldn't tolerate that feeling.

"So, what is it you want from me?" she asked with exasperation. Her huge eyes were watching my face, as though trying to see something there that would answer her question. "We aren't alike, you know. Nothing alike. We come from different backgrounds and we have different goals. You have your responsibilities and I have mine. None of those are in common."

"Gwen, listen to me. This isn't a casual flirtation if that's what you were thinking."

"Of course, that's what I'm thinking. Men like you do not associate with women like me."

"You keep saying that. What is it about you that makes you so afraid?"

"Okay, you want to know? Fine. I'll show you. Then you'll understand. And when you see, you'll leave me alone forever. I won't be insulted, I won't be hurt, I already prepared myself for that outcome. Park this car and come with me." Her voice was adamant and emotional. I had no idea what it was she was hiding, but I knew I was about to find out.

Chapter 10

Gwen

I'd done everything that I could to discourage Colt Stillman from becoming a part of my life. I didn't have the luxury of letting him toy with my affections. I knew a hundred girls who would've taken one look at him or at his bank account, and jumped in the seat next to him, ready to take the ride no matter where it ended as he dumped them. I was different. I had a child, had responsibilities. I had a career in the making and these were the only things that would keep Carrie and me from living on the streets, probably Bitsy as well. I had to protect us all. I could not afford the risk that was called Colt Stillman.

Nevertheless, there I was, taking him to the door of my apartment building. He stood back at the bottom of the steps as I unlocked the outer door and opened it. He reached over my head and held the door open as I went through and started up the stairs. "Come along. You may as well see it at its beautiful best," I said sarcastically. We trudged past Mrs. Heathrow's apartment. She was collecting her newspaper and waved to me briefly. I just smiled and kept going upstairs. I didn't have time for introductions and she'd never see him again, so it didn't matter.

The second floor led to the third and that's where

Bitsy and I lived with Carrie. The sound of my key in the door alerted Bitsy that I was home. I opened the door, pushed it open, and swept my arm wide to invite Colt in. Bitsy was standing in the little kitchenette, her hair still tousled from the day. She was getting ready for work and the sight of Colt in our tiny apartment took her by surprise, to say the least. Walking behind me, he came in and stood to one side. I took the opportunity to shut the door and slide off my coat, but he beat me to it. He took my coat and laid it over the back of a chair, removing his own and rubbing his hands together.

"Well, Bitsy, we meet again. It seems I've arrived at an inopportune time. I apologize for that, but it couldn't be helped. Gwenn's car wouldn't start, and I brought her home."

Bitsy was puzzled. "You just happened by when her car wouldn't start?"

That was when it hit me. I turned around slowly, my mouth gaping in amazement. "You. You did it, didn't you?"

He didn't bother to deny it, I had to give him that. "I'm a very determined man when I want something, Gwen. If it means disarming your car for a couple of hours, so be it. It's worth it even if you are mad at me because I'm here now and that's where I want to be."

Bitsy shook her head. "Oh, no, this is where I exit. She

grabbed her coat, her purse, and a hairbrush in her hand as she left the apartment. Then it was just Colt, Carrie, and me.

Carrie pulled herself to a stand in the playpen. Drool running from the corner of her mouth signaled the incoming tooth that kept her fussy.

"Well, who have we here?"

"That's Carrie," I said solemnly, framing my next sentence.

Colt walked over to the playpen, bent low and picked Carrie up, putting her on his shoulder. "What a pretty little thing you are. And you look so lonely in that playpen. If I weren't so heavy, I'd climb in there with you and then we could both play together." He smiled at her and she reached up to pinch the dimple in his cheek. He was much larger than any man she'd seen before, and I was surprised she wasn't afraid. They say children know who to trust, and maybe it was that instinct that made her smile in his company.

"You know, I think she kind of likes me."

"Don't get ahead of yourself. She's like that with everyone." At that exact moment, Carrie burst out in a squall.

"It would seem that she's not like that with *everyone*,

now wouldn't it?" His expression was sardonic and infuriating.

I didn't know what to say, so I sputtered the first thing that came to mind. "That's Bitsy's daughter, you know. They're staying here with me and we share watching the child. Bitsy has to work at night and of course, daycare is hard to come by. It works for both of us." I walked to the kitchen at, opened the cupboard and pulled two cups out, setting the kettle on the stove to make hot water for tea. "I suppose you will drink a cup with me?"

"Of course. He walked around the coffee table and sat down on the sofa, patting Carrie on the back to calm her. I went toward them, and Carrie's arms instantly reached out to me. "Mama, Mama," she attempted to say. It was her first words and she been practicing them for the past week.

"Oh, Carrie, honey. You know I'm not your mommy." I took Carrie from him and added, "She gets confused, you know? She has Bitsy during the day and me at night. It's no wonder she doesn't know her mother is."

Cole nodded, his face passive. "Do you sleep here on the sofa?"

"Oh, no, I sleep in the bedroom with Carrie." As soon as the words were out of my mouth, I knew I'd been trapped. He knew very well that Carrie was mine, but he wasn't calling me a liar. There was something about him that kept tugging at my heart. I wanted to think he was such a bully, a demon and a thoughtless man who was just after sex, and yet, time after time, he was proving me wrong. I couldn't put him in the same column as Paul. There were few comparisons between the two. This was confusing, and I didn't know what to say. The entire atmosphere felt awkward to me.

I flushed and handed Carrie back to him as the teakettle began to whistle. Colt looked quite comfortable, playing with Carrie. I soon appeared with two cups of hot tea, put Carrie in her playpen and sat on the sofa next to him.

"So, now, is this it? Your daughter? Is that what you are afraid of people finding out?"

I was frustrated, caught in my lie and feeling questioned at the same time. "Well, of course! Wouldn't you be?"

He shook his head. "Not necessarily, Gwen. You're assuming that I don't have the capacity to care about you if you have a child. Don't you think that's a little judgmental?"

He had a point. "I have to protect her. She's all I have. I'm all she has. It's not just you, there are the people I work for, too. But, I must admit, it's mostly you."

"I understand that I really do. But I don't suppose it

ever occurred to you that I would never come between you and your child. You and your daughter are a package deal and if I'm pursuing you, that means she's part of you. Do you understand?"

I nodded and sipped my cup. It was hot, and the liquid felt good going down. I knew Carrie was going to begin crying for her bottle at any moment and I hoped she would squall loudly so he would leave. I was uncomfortable in the tiny space that I called home and that wasn't right. I wish I hadn’t made the tea. It suggested that I wanted him to stay and I really didn't.

Chapter 11

Coulter

I'd suspected for some time that the child was behind Gwen's reluctance to have anything to do with me. I'd known about the baby. Bitsy had confessed to Buddy, and he had relayed the news to me. I had known with every instinct that she would be a wonderful mother. Even so, she had seemed so single and available. I supposed it was the close relationship between Bitsy and her that allowed them to coordinate so well. They were both able to live lives as young women, even though there was a child involved. I liked children. I hoped to have some of my own someday.

The baby began to cry, and Gwen put her cup down on the coffee table. "Excuse me, I have to make her bottle and put her down to sleep." I knew she expected me to recognize my cue to leave, but I didn't want to. I'd gone through too much with her to leave now. It was a tender, almost family moment and I wanted to stay, I wanted to be a part of it. So, I watched as she prepared the bottle and carried it along with Carrie into the bedroom. I could hear her humming a lullaby as she changed the baby's clothing. I got up and stood in the doorway, watching her. She kissed the baby fondly on both cheeks and cuddled her against her face before putting the bottle into her mouth and laying her down in the crib. She gently tucked covers up around her and added a little green elephant that waited at the foot of the crib. I studied the crib and then the bed where Gwen slept at night. It was a tiny room and the bed was no bigger than a twin. I wondered how she slept in it, given that she was tall, but I knew that having her daughter close by was more important than her own comfort. Once the baby was happily sucking at the bottle, Gwen turned, and putting a finger to her mouth to silence me, she came toward me and motioned me out the doorway. She pulled the door shut behind herself and looked at me as if to say, are you leaving now?

"I have an idea," I said. "I know a nice little restaurant not too far from here. If you'll allow me, I'd like to call and order some dinner for us. Will you let me do that for you?"

There was a mixed look on her face. I saw the fleeting glance of gratitude that meant she wouldn't have to cook, or maybe she was planning on eating something simple like scrambled eggs and didn't have anything to offer me. On the other hand, she wanted to tell me no, to tell me to go away and leave her in her predicament. She didn't understand me. She might never understand me, but that didn't mean I would stop trying. "What do you say?"

She nodded, and I didn't give her enough time to change her mind. I pulled out my phone and ordered us two steak dinners with all the trimmings. We settled back on the sofa and she flipped on the television using the remote. She settled on a show from National Geographic, something that was neutral and interesting. She kept the sound low and I was grateful for that. I had the idea she wanted to talk it out.

There came a knock at the door and she went to answer it. It was the restaurant. Evidently, someone had let the man in downstairs. The waiter brought in several boxes and looked to Gwen for some indication where he was to lay out the dinner. I saw a fleeting glance of alarm in her eyes and she motioned to the coffee table. There was no dining room. He nodded as if it was the most natural thing in the world and cleared away the remote and the short pile of magazines that lay there. With a sweep of his hand, he snapped a white linen tablecloth over the coffee table, tucking it inward so that it looked almost as if it were made for it. He looked at Gwen again and she realized he wanted plates. She pulled two unmatched plates from the cupboard and handed them to him, following those with flatware and paper towels to use as napkins. The waiter set out the various boxes, filling our plates and I had to give him credit: for what he had to work with, he made it look five-star. I tipped him well and he nodded and left quietly. There was a bottle of wine and I lightened the mood by grabbing our empty teacups from the side table where the waiter had set them. I poured some wine and each of the cups and handed one to her. She smiled and gave me a half nod. I knew she understood.

I was famished, so it was very little effort for me to

begin eating. She began picking, but soon her nervousness must have dwindled because she picked up her steak knife and began cutting hearty chunks of the meat.

"Bitsy would absolutely kill me if she knew I was having steak," she said with a guilty tone.

"Then, next time I come I will make sure that Bitsy's home and include her. Who knows? Maybe we'll invite Buddy along."

"Have you forgiven Bitsy for her involvement in that elevator fiasco?" she asked me.

I waved my hand from side to side. "All forgotten," I murmured and sipped the wine. I could feel it coursing through my veins, calming me down. As self-assured as I was, the close call of losing her permanently had me shaking to my knees.

We ate in silence for a while, enjoying the delicious food. The television show fascinated us as we watched a lioness prowling. The announcer was commenting that it was the male's job to hunt but, in this case, the lioness was left alone with the cubs. "This reminds me of my boss, Metallica," she said conversationally. "She came to the US as a child. Her father worked for the United Nations and eventually, she ended up here in Chicago. She's one tough lady, smart and savvy. I'm learning a lot from her."

"Do you really enjoy your job?"

"I'm lucky to have it," she nodded. "I could be working in fast food."

I nodded in agreement and picked up my teacup of wine. I held it out toward her. "To us," I toasted. She hesitated only a moment but lifted her cup to tap against mine and we both sipped the sweet liquid, thereby sealing our intentions.

"You know, you've never answered me." She put the comment out there and I knew she wanted an answer.

"About?"

"What is it you want from me? Now you know my truth. I'm an unmarried mother with a child and I must work and live in this tiny little apartment with a girlfriend to get by. I'm not in your group, Colt. I don't move in your circles, and quite frankly, I'm not sure I want to."

"Somewhere along the line, you've got a really bad opinion of people with money. How do you see the world so black-and-white?"

She shrugged. "I didn't use to," she said softly. "Things happen that teach you lessons along the way. I learned one of those lessons."

I let it go. She deserved to have some secrets, but maybe someday she would open enough to share them with me.

Chapter 12

Gwen

I had to give the devil his due. Colt seemed to have a way of seeing through me. He could tell I was holding back, but he was patient, at least to a certain extent. He was completely right. I had run out on him, and that wasn't something he deserved. He'd been nothing but kind to me. I realized then, with a certain amount of shock, that the entire conflict between Colt and myself was my own doing. I was the one with the hasty condemnation, based on someone else entirely. I was the one with headstrong goals that weren't practical. Worse yet, I had closed off my normally loving, generous, emotional heart to all males in general. In short, I was bitter. How could I set that example for my daughter? How could she ever hope to find a fulfilling, loving relationship with a man when my actions, body language, and disposition told her to stay away? When had I become so judgmental?

These realizations did not come easily to me. In school, things had seemed to always work out in my behalf. I got used to it, assuming that they were testimony to the fact that I was right. How foolish was that? Things also work out for people who are bad and wrong. Paul Romano was such an example. For that matter, take the man who was there beside me at that moment. To my knowledge, he'd never done anything to hurt anyone and yet he was on trial for having done just that. The worst part was, he had been set up and lies were told about him. The judge found him innocent, but society found him guilty. Or, was it only me who found him guilty?

He was watching me and while he couldn't guess as to the extent of what I was thinking, I believe he knew I was being thoughtful. And well I should be. I motioned to the sofa. "Would you sit back down for a few minutes before you leave?" I knew he hadn't mentioned leaving, but there were always certain points in conversation, little milestones where both parties find it polite to express their appreciation and take their leave. This was one of those points, but I decided I didn't want him to go quite yet.

"Sure," he smiled and sat down, extending a hand in my direction to bring me down next to him. How could he be so continually affable when I had treated him so poorly? Now was my time to remedy that.

"I think I may owe you an apology," I said quietly to which he snapped his head and shoulders backward, mocking me with incredulity. "No, no I really mean that. You've pointed out all along that I've made you my enemy and for no good reason. I don't know what it is, maybe your being here and maybe your being around Carrie, but I think you're right. Something happened, and I won't go into details, but it took away the innocence and trust I felt for others. To be very honest, I didn't see it in myself. You were the one who pointed it out. I owe you for that. For what it's worth, I'm sorry. You've given more than what's been fair to me and I haven't given much back if anything." I didn't know what else to say. The words came hard and this surprised me. I'd always been so easy going. Somewhere I had grown hard inside and that made speaking difficult as it always is when you're wrong.

"Thank you for that. I will be very honest with you. I'm not a man who's been known for his kindness, rather his efficiency and determination."

I laughed. "Determination? No, say it isn't so," I teased him.

"Nevertheless, you opened up a little and I think it is only fair that I open up likewise. So, what I'm admitting to you, is that maybe I should have pulled back and respected your boundaries better. I aggravated whatever was bothering you and that didn't help things. But all that said, I want to be with you. I don't want to be with anyone else. I'm guessing you're afraid that I'll see you as a conquest and once you've surrendered, then I'll grow bored and move on?"

"You do have that reputation."

He was silent for a few long moments and then said in a very soft voice, "Someone did that to you once, didn't they?"

I looked at the floor but couldn't bring myself to nod. It was too humiliating, and the memories hurt as they flooded back into the front of my consciousness. He reached over and tapped my arm lightly.

"It's okay. We don't need to talk about it. But that doesn't change what I said. I do want to be with you, and I am determined person. So, I'm going to pull you over and kiss you now. I'm giving you advanced warning, so you can bolt from the room if necessary," he grinned, mocking me, "but I sincerely hope that you choose to stay put. Here we go now, here's the countdown, 3-2-1!"

I saw his hands move toward me and felt them as they grabbed my upper arms pulling me gently, but steadily toward him. I looked up at him, questioning, but his eyes were already closed as he bent and kissed me. It wasn't a simple or chaste kiss but one filled with desire and masculine triumph. What had begun as a lighthearted exchange had quickly boiled into a thick, heated need for one another. We entered that other world, the one without time or consequence. I never felt his hands as they pulled my shirt over my head or slid down the zipper of my skirt. All I knew was that I wanted him naked. The lamplight in the room was dim, and I looked at his body as he sat facing me. His shoulders were muscled and wide and tapered to a narrow waist. His upper arms were fluid extensions of his muscled chest, the veins standing up slightly from the skin. He had a ghost of a shadowy beard, mostly along the sides of his cheeks. I realized how sexy that was and wanted to feel those whiskers against my smooth skin. His brilliant blue eyes contrasted with the black hair that now had fallen forward, and they delivered a tantalizing, sexy look. And then my eyes traveled lower.

There was no mistaking that he felt the need, and that need was for me. His penis was fully erect, the veins standing out as the blood coursed through it, making it pulse with desirability. In some strange, primitive way, I couldn't help myself, but I lunged forward and put my hands around it, feeling him jerk from the sudden contact. Instead of pulling away, his hips moved toward me, as though he wanted to penetrate me without further delay. I put one hand on his chest and shook my head. "No, let me."

His eyes widened at the import of what I was saying. I bent down and placed my tongue on his reddened tip, running it around the circumference before sliding it into my mouth. I could feel the pulsing increase and he tasted slightly salty. I'd never done anything like that before and I wondered if I was doing it correctly. I open one eye as I quickly glanced at him. His eyes were half-shuttered, his head rolled back in passion. I let instinct take over. In that world we'd entered where there was no time, there was no accountability for the actions that followed. We only managed quick flashes of awareness, as when I realized what I needed to do to him, he felt he needed to do likewise. We fell upon each other's bodies, exploring with tongues and lips and fingers that felt for responses and then revisited to increase the desire until neither of us could stand it any longer. There was a flash of realization as I felt him enter me, gently and yet with an insistence that I couldn't deny. He fed me with himself, stroking me inside of my vaginal walls, twisting his hips so as not to miss an iota of tender flesh. He drove slowly, but insistently, from time to time stiffening when he reached my terminus. It felt exquisite.

There wasn't much room to maneuver on that little sofa of ours, but Colt made the most of it, consuming me from above. His hands fed my full breasts into his mouth and there, his lips and sucking tongue took over. Every time the tip of his tongue brushed my nipple, it was soft, creating a feathery explosion in my depths. He followed that with another stroke, the off-and-on contrast between the two driving my mind and senses into a sphere that hovered somewhere above us. I didn't think about recriminations, I didn't think about anything but Colt and what he was doing to me. I raised my hips to meet each thrust. I couldn't seem to get him deep enough or the flesh of our groins flat enough against one another to feel fulfilled. Perhaps that was the way it was intended, that the act was built of desire and lack of fulfillment. No, I was wrong, in those next moments, I felt the pressure building somewhere in my hips, the stimulation against the soft flesh of my clitoris. He was very aware of what he was doing to me, indeed I opened my eyes and saw him watching my face. He alternated in depth, in speed, and in the amount of flesh that touched between us. His hands came down and lifted my buttocks to an angle that allowed him to penetrate me more deeply, more rapidly and with greater finesse. Then we entered that world where the sky is filled with stars, you're not aware of breathing but only the exquisite breaking of shudders as they ripple through your body, making you convulse as you give in to them. I looked at his face briefly, his head thrown back, the muscles in his neck standing out and throbbing as he found his own world beyond. He jerked and held his body rigid, unwilling to interrupt their flow until they had subsided.

Colt opened his eyes and looked at me then and we exchanged a knowing glance. It was a look of lovers who recognized they'd found their partner in all things. Colt's arms came down and slid beneath my back, lifting me as he rolled me atop him. I laid there along the length of his body, his skin damp from exertion. We were both breathing heavily, and he wrapped his arms tightly around me as well as his heavy leg and thigh encasing me as much as possible. We needed that touch. We needed that closeness, that lack of separation. We fought for it.

After some time, the ecstasy passed and we returned to our bodies. There was a short, uncomfortable moment when we realized there was nowhere else to go but down, back into our bodies, back into that awkward routine of conversation between us. He kissed me to ease the passing, and I wanted to climb into his skin and stay there with him forever.

Finally, I pushed at his chest and softly asked him to let me get up. In one movement, I rose to my feet, my hands lifting my heavy hair and rolling it into a bun tucked at the back of my head. My body needed ventilation, the sheen of perspiration and residual warmth from his body begged for cool air. I knew what I wanted but was hesitant; would he misunderstand?

"Would you like to take a shower with me?" I asked tentatively.

He didn't misunderstand; he didn't think I was trying to wash his fluids from my skin. We both wanted to feel fresh and clean and so he nodded and followed me and we crowded into the tiny standup shower. We took turns soaping one another's bodies and laughed as I tried to wash his thighs, but the cramped space caused me to slip and fall to the bottom of the shower stall.

He laughed loudly and bent to rescue me, lifting me up off my feet. He kissed my thighs and my womanhood and up the trail of my body to my nipples and into that soft space in my throat that throbbed when he made love to me. He slowly allowed me down to my feet and then wrapped his body around me.

"I wanted you so badly," he said softly, and I nodded,

knowing.

We finally shut off the cooling water and wrapped in towels, taking turns drying one another's backs. He began pulling on his clothes and I went into the small bedroom, peered at Carrie and then drew a sleep shirt and a pair of fresh panties from the drawer. "I'm sorry, but I can't invite you to stay. There just isn't any room."

"I know," he said in a resigned tone. "But it was wonderful, you're wonderful, and I want you more right now than I did before."

His words were reassuring and made me feel safe and wanted. I let them settle down over me like a warm furry robe.

"I'm going to leave you now," he said. "I will see you tomorrow, so get in there and get a good night's sleep." His voice was teasing in a pseudo-parent's way. I nodded in response. Both of us seemed to hesitate to go back into that verbal world where we crossed swords. For the moment we were content, we were together, and it was enough.

He went to the door, opened it, and turned to say, "I will see you tomorrow." I nodded, and he left. I skipped over to the door and placed my ear against the wood, listening to his footsteps as he descended the three flights of stairs until he reached the ground. I scooted to the window and watched him leave, climbing into his car and pulling into traffic and then finally he was nothing more than a pair of taillights that blended in with all the others. Sad that he was gone, I hugged myself and climbed beneath the covers of my bed. With a deep sigh, I was soon asleep.

Chapter 13

Coulter

I hated leaving Gwen. Her daughter was adorable, and I'd felt something unique when I held her. As an only child, I'd never been around children. It triggered something in me. I knew what Gwen triggered in me; that was completely clear.

I couldn't figure out why she found it necessary to hide Carrie from me, and from others. I supposed she still carried her small-town stigma about single mothers. I knew she never married the father. It was one of the things I checked.

I decided to drive around the city before I went back to the condo. I felt restless, an unfamiliar feeling for someone whose workload was always quadruple what normal men worked. I did it deliberately. I had plans of being a permanent bachelor and whatever women would come and go through my life would be temporary. Now I was feeling a draw toward one single woman, and this was a totally new experience for me. It felt like things were moving quickly, almost dizzily, but that's who I was. When I set my mind to something, I wasted no time. Too many things, really good things, had been lost due to hesitation. I had no plans of losing Gwen, ever.

I drove toward the lakeshore and found a vantage point where I could park looking out over the water. I could see boats making port in the distance and there was even a flash of lightning as a storm was approaching from the west. I decided at that moment that I would buy a boat, one large enough to handle the rough waters of Lake Michigan and sleep a half-dozen people. I knew nothing about boating, but I could hire people who did. I would take Gwen and Carrie with me. Hell, I would even invite Buddy and that ditzy Bitsy roommate. We could go up the coast on both states, making port in towns that looked interesting. I'd heard there were some beautiful sightseeing locations along Lake Superior. I decided I would begin looking the next day and felt a little excited at the anticipation.

My cell buzzed in my pocket and I quickly grabbed it, thinking it was Gwen calling to tell me good night. It was a number I didn't recognize, and I came close to sending it to voicemail. It was my private number, though, and unless someone had misdialed accidentally, I had no idea who it would be. Then came one of those little voice moments that told me to take the call.

"Hello?"

"Is this Colt Stillman?"

"Who is calling please?"

"I'm sorry, but the law requires I verify that this is

Colt Stillman." I was puzzled, it wasn't as if they could serve you legal papers over the phone.

"Yes, this is he. With whom am I speaking?"

"Mr. Stillman, your name and number are listed as emergency contacts for Mr. William Clark?"

"Buddy! What's wrong?"

"Mr. Stillman, your friend has been involved in a very serious automobile accident. My name is Mrs. Green and I am a social worker at Mount Mercy Hospital. We are trying to locate a next of kin or emergency contact individual to come in. Would you be available?"

"Oh, shit! Is he alive?"

"Mr. Stillman, I apologize, but I'm unable to release any personal information over the telephone. I would need you to come in with a picture ID. I'm sure you understand."

"Dammit, tell me! Is he still alive?"

"The only thing I can say, Mr. Stillman, is that I am not calling you for mortuary services. Does that help?"

"Where do I find you?"

"Give them your name at the emergency desk and they'll page me. That's Mrs. Green, Marjorie Green. I'll expect to see you soon."

I already had the car in reverse and spun out getting onto to the road. Luckily, Mount Mercy wasn't far and it was late, so the traffic was light. I swung into the emergency parking and sprinted through the doors to the reception desk. "Mrs. Green, I'm here to see her. Tell her it's Colt Stillman. She's expecting me."

"Please have a seat in that first conference room on the left and she'll be in to see you," the woman there said, pointing down the hallway. I looked around the waiting room quickly but there was no one there I recognized. I must have been Buddy's only emergency contact. I found the room and went in, pacing until the Green woman came in.

"Won't you have a seat, Mr. Stillman?"

"I'd rather stand if you don't mind," I told her firmly.

"If you wish, but I have some papers for you to sign. That might be easier if you're seated."

I felt a sick dread in my gut and did as she asked. Whipping out my wallet, I extracted my license and slid it across the table toward her. "My picture ID," I commented.

She took it and stood, clasping it in her hand. "I need to copy this, I'll be right back."

Jesus, this is like being in court! I knew I was agitated. Why the hell couldn't the woman just tell me what shape he was in? She was back in a matter of moments according to the clock on the wall, although it felt like hours. Why did every hospital room have a clock? To tally your misery?

Mrs. Green slid my license back across the table. "Thank you, hospital rules and I understand your frustration. Your friend, Mr. Clark is alive. He was involved in an accident earlier this evening and paramedics were forced to extract him from his vehicle with cutting equipment. From what I understand, his car rolled over an embankment a number of times and he was unconscious when he was brought in. I really don't have any more information than that for you right now because I'm not medically qualified to give you diagnosis or prognosis. You will, however, be able to speak to the doctors. Mr. Clark is still being examined and treatment determined."

I heaved a sigh that he was alive... for the time being. "Where is he?"

"He is still in the ER, pending tests and I suspect will be either sent to surgery or ICU depending on the results and what sort of treatment is required. I will not candy coat this, Mr. Stillman. Your friend is in very critical condition—I've seen the charts often enough to note that. He has not regained consciousness as far as I'm aware. We found this card in his wallet while looking for identification." She held it up and I recognized his Stillman Enterprises business card. She turned it over and there was handwriting on the back.

"May I?"

"Of course," and she handed it over.

Essentially it was Buddy's request that I be contacted and treated as medical power of attorney in case of emergency. He had no other family. He listed Mason's phone number for the documentation, including a DNR requesting that life-saving measures beyond immediate requirements not be provided. I was blown away. His entire life was in my hands and his wishes stipulated on the back of a lousy business card.

"Mr. Stillman, you should know that Mr. Clark's license is marked giving permission for his participation in the donor program, should he not survive."

"Don't!"

"I'm sorry?"

"Don't say those words to me. Not now. Buddy is flesh and blood and like a brother to me. He has a hundred people who care about him, even if they aren't blood relations. Do not refer to him as a corpse in your donor kitchen, do you understand?"

"But, Mr. Stillman, it's important..."

"I said, do-not! If your services are required by me, I will let you know. In the meantime, I want to talk to the doctors and I will be consulting with a few of my own."

"Mr. Stillman, doctors must have privileges with Mount Mercy to be able to treat patients here. That's the law."

"Then I'll move him out. Whatever. Now, let me see him and his doctors."

I knew I was being a jerk, but I'd learned how to deal with places like hospitals. You had to put your foot down and be assertive otherwise they'd wander around at their own pace and bombard you with rules designed to raise your tab while they practiced with their diagnostic toys. That wasn't going to happen to Buddy—not on my watch.

"Mr. Stillman, if you will... there are a number of papers here we need you to sign."

"What are they?"

"Mostly permissions for treatment, release of liability, the standard forms patients sign on admission."

"Hold on to them. My attorney will be here shortly,

and I will bring in my own people as second opinions."

"Mr. Stillman, you do realize that we can't proceed with treatment unless these forms are signed?"

I slammed my hand on the table and leaned over it, coming close to her face. I could tell she was alarmed and I didn't give a shit. "Now listen. I don't know you and you probably haven't heard of me. We don't run in the same circles, you and I. I will tell you this, however. There is a wing in this hospital that my family paid to have built. We endorsed major equipment acquisition here for treating children. In short, Ms. Green, your administrator will not be happy with the way I'm being treated. I don't give a rat's ass about your rules. My best friend in the world is in that ER of yours and you *will* treat him, with or without my signature on these god-damned papers, do you understand? My attorney will be here in a matter of minutes when I make the call, and you can expect the best and the brightest doctors to be arriving shortly thereafter. Why? Because *they*, Ms. Green, *do* know who I am and not to interfere with me or my orders. Have I made myself clear?"

Whether she responded from fear, or realization of the truth I spoke, it didn't matter. Time was passing, and I didn't know how much Buddy had left. "Go!" I shooed her away and slid out my cell.

I called Mason and while I waited for him to arrive, I

made a few calls to friends of my father's who were tops in their fields. Several were at Mayo and I sent my corporate jet to pick them up. They could be on site in a matter of a couple of hours. I hoped Buddy had that long.

Mrs. Green left the consultation room and returned, a visitor's pass in her hand. "This will get you into his room but stay out of the way and do what the nurses tell you to," she said briefly and left. I figured she was out of the way for the time being.

Pushing through the double doors, I found the cubicle marked on the pass and staggered when I saw Buddy. He was on a ventilator and his head almost totally bandaged. As I came closer to the bed, I could see his features were badly bruised and swollen beyond recognition. If I hadn't known where to find him, I would have passed this man by. A bank of equipment with lights and beeps surrounded him and his arms sprouted a dozen or so wires from beneath the blankets. He was a fucking mess!

A nurse came in and looked at me, so I pulled out the pass. "Only a couple of minutes. We're getting ready to take him for a CT scan."

"I'd like to see his doctors," I told her.

"I'm sorry. They're with other patients right now and they really can't tell you anything until the tests results are back. Now, if you'll step out, Mr. Stillman, was it? I need to check his bandages for seepage and this won't be pleasant."

"I can take it. I'm not going anywhere."

She looked doubtful, but shrugged and nodded, turning to her work. I backed off and stood in the far corner out of her way. She was right—it was a helluva nasty sight. I couldn't imagine that Buddy was still alive, given what I saw.

When she finally left the room, I stepped closer to the bed. He was unconscious and, on a ventilator, but I bent low and whispered to him. "Buddy, it's me, Colt. I'm here and I'm not leaving. I've got the big guys on the way and they're going to make sure you're up and around in time to come to work on Monday, you hear? Just relax—I've got this."

The words rang loudly in my head. That's what Buddy always said to me, "I've got this." Well, it was my turn.

Chapter 14

Gwen

I awakened with sunshine emanating from my soul. I never thought I could feel that happy again. In fact, it was better than it could have ever been with Paul. I was in love, but it was on my terms. It doesn't get any better than that.

Carrie seemed to sense my light mood and pulled up on the side of the crib and clearly said, "Mama." I was thrilled and swept her into my arms as I headed for the kitchen to make our breakfasts.

Bitsy was groggy on the sofa. She normally didn't get in until one or two in the morning, so I let her sleep. It was tough to be quiet with a baby and an open kitchenette that never had enough room for noisy pans. Carrie, having mastered her vocabulary, was repeating "Mama" over and over. I sat her in her high chair and gave her some small bits of grapes and a warm bottle of oatmeal. I broke two eggs into the warped frying pan and I think the smell of breakfast is what got Bitsy off the sofa.

"Hi," she greeted me, sitting up on the sofa, rubbing her eyes and turning in my direction. "Is that my girl calling for Mama?" she chortled to Carrie.

"We've created a monster, I'm afraid. She thinks she

has two mamas and of course you know what that makes other people think."

Bitsy's head cocked to one side. "Never thought of it like that."

"So, listen, as soon as these eggs are done, I'm off to work. Metallica has some consultants coming in from some of our bigger lines and I've been asked to sit in. It's sort of a pain, but more of an honor. I'm going to run late tonight, so I'll check in with Mrs. Heathrow and make sure she can take Carrie off your hands when you leave for work."

"Works for me. I'm headed to the bathroom and then I'll fry myself some eggs. That smells good."

I nodded and soon scooted Carrie into my arms and got her ready for the day, my eyes glued to the clock. Colt had promised to call, and he knew I had to be at work. I sort of expected him to have already texted me or something.

I put Carrie in the playpen and slid on my shoes.

Bitsy was fully awake and looking around. "I noticed some fancy trash in the kitchen. You have company?"

"You know very well who," I grinned and said.

"We need another bedroom."

"I couldn't agree more," I said and winked as I left.

Chapter 15

Coulter

Although I had the best people money could buy, it was pure anguish to watch Buddy lie there, unconscious with me unable to help him. I wracked my brain to come up with solutions. I had the jet standing by and could have flown him anywhere in the world if it would have helped. My doctors told me he was too fragile to be moved and after consulting with the staff doctor at Mount Mercy, they assured me he was in the best situation possible and only time would make the difference in his outcome.

I wasn't allowed to sit in the ICU room with him, and I understood that. I took up post, instead, in the family waiting room on the same hall. While his body had sustained cuts and skeletal damage, it was his head injury that caused the greatest concern. When they came in to tell me they were taking him into the operating room to drill a hole through his skull, I thought it was all over. They explained they were releasing pressure from the swelling and even if he made it through the surgery, they would keep him in a coma to put the least demands on his body. I paced and thought and then repeated it. Finally, it occurred to me that Bitsy should know and perhaps it could even be a good influence for him to hear her voice. I texted her and in less than forty-five minutes she came into the waiting room, little Carrie in a stroller and a diaper bag over her shoulder. “They won’t let me in to see him,” she told me.

I nodded. “I know. They’re about to take him into surgery and release pressure from the swelling on his brain. I’m sorry about all this,” I said, motioning to the room in which we sat, “but they tell me he can’t be moved elsewhere so this is what we have to work with.”

Bitsy followed by glance and looked around. “I’m sorry? I don’t understand what’s wrong?”

I realized that to Bitsy, this rather unknown hospital was what she was accustomed to. I would have had him in a private suite at Mayo if they’d let me.

What the hell am I saying? What an ass I’ve turned into—an arrogant, privileged ass.

“What can I do?” Bitsy asked, her kindly eyes filled with empathy and dampness on her cheeks. *She’s really not so bad,* I thought. *She seems to really care about him.*

“Nothing, right now. It’s out of our hands.” I sat forward in my chair. “Look, Bitsy. Buddy has the best I can get for him. He’s going to get worse before he gets better—they tell me that’s normal. But he *will* come out of this—that much I promise you. Between you and I, we will bring him back if we have to suction his consciousness right out of his nostrils!”

She laughed at that and I was glad to see we could relax and be less morose. It made the waiting that much easier. That was a good thing because there was plenty of it to be done.

Chapter 16

Gwen

Metallica was in her element. She reigned like a queen over her subjects as the consultants fought for her attention and I stood by silently, doing her bidding and learning. I'd yet to ever see her smile, but the radiance on her face came as close to it as I suppose she was capable.

It was, however, exhausting. There was so much to remember and although I sat in the corner and furiously took notes, at some point it all began to run together.

I was having problems concentrating and Colt was the reason why. I'd emerged from my building that morning, having completely forgotten that my car was still marooned at work and not running. To my immense surprise, my car was sitting in the parking lot, clean, detailed and filled with gas. I used my spare key to open it and there was a gold keyring on the seat, inscribed with my initials. There was also a second set of keys and an envelope with my name on it.

"Stop by Waltham's on your way home. There's a little something there I want you to have. I don't want any strangers giving you rides home—they could decide they want to stay!"

I had no idea what kind of place Waltham's was, but it didn't matter because I was running late, and my car was safely in my hands. I turned the key and the engine answered like a knight on a white horse.

Colt had probably ordered that all done the day before, even before he slept with me. He had planned to leave me marooned, after all. Why wasn't he calling?

Then I knew.

He'd seen me—the real me. He'd seen where and how I lived in that shoddy, little, odd apartment with the cracks in the ceiling and tiny shower with rust stains. He knew he couldn't have me lugging Carrie around on my hip on dates and that he certainly wasn't going to spend the night at my place—not when the only place to sleep was half of a cramped bed with a young child staring over the crib railing at him.

Of course! What a fool I'd been! I'd allowed myself to forget, in the space of one cozy little evening, that men were all the same. They used you, like a cat toy. They flirted and bragged and promised, when all along, all they wanted to know was how good you were in bed and whether they should brag about you to their locker room buddies or try to forget they'd ever touched you.

When would I ever learn?

Metallica was looking in my direction and I could tell I'd been drifting mentally and not paying attention. I struggled to pick up the thread of conversation and realized the meeting had come to an end and she'd asked me to show out the guests. I scrambled to comply and as I shook hands and let the last one out the door, I turned around to see her glaring at me.

"You had better things to do?" she barked, and the store grew quiet as both customers and employees stopped what they were doing to hear me getting chewed out. I knew my face was flaming. This was all Stillman's fault—he'd gotten in the way of my career, just as Paul had ruined my dreams.

I choked back tears and felt my phone vibrating and then it stopped, only to repeat fifteen seconds later. It was Bitsy! Something was wrong and that was our signal to find a place and call.

I apologized to Metallica and pretended to cry so I could run to the ladies' room. She seemed appeased by my obedience and let me go, glaring at the others in the store to remind them who was queen.

I locked myself in a stall and quickly called Bitsy. "What is it? What's wrong? Is Carrie okay?"

"She's fine. I need you to come to Mount Mercy Hospital, fifth-floor waiting room. Buddy was in a car wreck and he's hurt bad. They've got him in surgery and you need to pick up Carrie and take her to Mrs. Heathrow's. Hurry."

Bitsy hung up and I was left there, my mouth open as I tried to absorb what she'd said. I washed my hands and emerged from the ladies' room, heading straight for Metallica's office. Tapping on the glass, she looked up and nodded for me to come in.

"I'm sorry to disturb you but I need to talk to you."

Her eyes widened and then narrowed. She thought I'd come to apologize and throw myself at her feet.

"I have to go, now. You never asked, and I have never shared that I have a baby, Metallica. My roommate and I work opposite shifts so she's cared for properly but there's been an emergency and I have to go and pick her up. I'm sorry I never told you and I'm sorry about what happened back there in the meeting. I know you're angry and I hope we can talk when I get back." The words spilled out of my mouth like an overflowing river—the flood getting broader and broader as I revealed more. Her response was blunt.

"Leave now."

I didn't stop to sort out whether that meant to leave now because I had trouble, or because she didn't want me to be there or come back. I'd have to figure it all later, but right then, I needed to get to my daughter and my best friend.

I pulled away from the curb distracted and a car honked behind me, letting me know I'd been careless. *Pull it together,* I told myself and headed toward the hospital. In the next second, I turned the corner, deciding to drop by the apartment which was only a couple of blocks away. I would pick up some extra things for Bitsy and pack a quick bag for Carrie. I'd also check in with Mrs. Heathrow. I hoped she'd take Carrie early, so I could go back and see if I still had a job.

It started to rain; great plops of water from over-burdened clouds and that only added to the dramatic misery I was about to live through.

Once upstairs, I stopped dead in my tracks.

Our apartment door was standing open. Bitsy hadn't left it that way in a hurry—no, this was more. Much more. At a glance, I could see the lock had been damaged and I poked my head around the door to peek inside. It was chaos. The kitchen drawers were pulled open and contents raked onto the floor. The sofa cushions overturned and slashed, their stuffing ripped into shreds on the carpet. My bedroom was a complete disaster: drawers overturned, bedding shredded into strips and worst of all, my beautiful new wardrobe had been slit into grossly barbaric pieces and the smell of urine was fresh and damp upon their cloth. The only things that weren't touched were those belonging to Carrie. Her crib, playpen, clothes and other necessities were untouched.

I stared in horror. This was not a random act by a

burglar. No, this was intentional and directly aimed at me. The fact that Carrie's possessions were left untouched spoke volumes. I could feel a panic begin to rise and knew that I didn't have the luxury of giving into it. I had to find the things I needed in the apartment and take them with me to the hospital. I needed to get to my daughter and not waste any more time. I grabbed an extra diaper bag, stuffing her little things into it. In the kitchen, I made some quick bottles for her and packed them into my baby cooler. The dresser where Bitsy kept her clothing had been rifled through, but nothing had been destroyed. Apparently, whoever had done this wasn't angry with her—they were angry with me. My hands shaking, I pulled together an extra set of clothes for her and threw them in a paper bag. My luggage in hand, I shut the door and locked it securely, although it was a joke since the lock had been destroyed.

Mrs. Heathrow said she would be only too glad to take Carrie early. I did not tell her about the mess upstairs. No one would discover it unless they went up there and the less said about it the time being, the better. I didn't have time to make a police report or to clean up the mess.

As I drove to the hospital, the few names of people I knew in town rolled through my mind. Obviously, Bitsy and her boyfriend, Buddy, were out of the question. That left our small group of friends we partied with, but nothing had happened recently that would've triggered that sort of invasion. I was down to the people at work. Most of the salespeople were on an as-needed basis, polite and supportive as far as work went. I knew this was beneath Metallica and after all, she had been with me when it probably took place.

That left one person, and only one. That left the one person who could not take no for an answer from me. That one person inserted himself continually in my private life. That man overrode my decisions in favor of his own and he was entirely casual in getting what he wanted. Was this some left-handed attempt to make me more dependent on him? I remembered the note he'd left on the car seat. I looked up the name of the company he told me to visit. Waltham's, as I remembered. The note was still lying in the seat next to me and as I drove, I double checked the name and then used the search function on my cell phone while sitting at a stoplight to track it down.

It was a Mercedes dealership. The man had bought me a car. I knew it as sure as I was sitting there, my hands shaking as the realization that I had once again lost control of my life began to sink in on me. I was in serious trouble this time. This man was powerful—he had connections and could make anything happen. He never bragged, but I knew. There was just that way about him. His people were connected; he was a man who knew how to use money. And I was his target. The horror of my predicament left me breathless.

I pulled into the parking lot of Mount Mercy Hospital, found an empty place, and picked up the bag with Bitsy's belongings. I went inside and up to the fifth floor as she had instructed me. There was a pair of double swinging doors at the end of the hallway with a large sign that denied admittance. Just before the door was a small room with a glass wall, and as I approached, I saw Bitsy sitting in one of the chairs, her legs crossed and her face in her hands. I knew Buddy was still alive or she would not have been waiting.

"Bitsy! How's Buddy? Are you holding up? Come here to Mama, Baby," I said, holding out my arms to take Carrie. I heard a male clearing his throat and turned around to see the man who had just destroyed our apartment sitting in the same room!

My hands began to shake, and I could only stare at him, trying to read his face, define any sign of why he had done it. He was extremely intelligent and a gifted actor, that much I knew. *He's got to know I've been by the house, doesn't he? Maybe not.* He looked exhausted and was wearing the same clothes he'd worn the night before with me. I knew I had to respond somehow if only to keep them calm until I could escape. I nodded. "Hello. How is Buddy? It's great that you're here for him. Do you know what happened?"

He must've felt the force field I was sending out to keep him away because he stood but didn't approach me.

"Hi. It seems like weeks since I've seen you. I got the call last night on my way home," he explained. "I don't know too many details about the accident, but his car flipped several times down an embankment and they had to cut them out."

I heard Bitsy gasp behind me. Obviously, that was the first she'd heard about it. "I'm so glad they got him out in time. How badly is he hurt?"

Colt shook his head. "We don't know. They've taken him into surgery and he'll be in there for a while. They're drilling a hole to release the pressure from his brain swelling, but they need to keep him in there in case that doesn't work, and they need to do more. I've only just gotten back. Bitsy stayed to be on hand, but I went to grab some breakfast. I'm glad you're here. Carrie shouldn't be in this place."

More like you went to grab some things in my apartment, I thought to myself but said, "She's going with me now." I turned to look at Bitsy. "Listen, I'll keep Carrie with me or make other arrangements. You don't worry about anything. Just be here for Buddy. I'll take care of the rest." She had no idea of the significance of my last sentence. It was my job to protect her, just as I did Carrie. I would clean up the apartment and she would never know what happened. I had no way to prove what I believed had taken place, and engaging Stillman at this point could prove rather dangerous. "Well, give Buddy a kiss for me. I need to go."

Without another word, I took the carriage handle and wheeled Carrie down the hallway toward the elevators. I heard my name called behind me. It was Stillman. The elevators opened, and I pushed the carriage inside, pretending I hadn't heard. My escape had just begun.

I parked Carrie with Mrs. Heathrow, telling her that I was going to paint our apartment and it would be better if Carrie wasn't in the fumes. Her face was puzzled but she didn't ask any questions and I didn't offer any further explanations. Step one had begun.

I pulled the box of large trash bags from beneath the kitchen sink and started in my room. With a broken heart, I gathered the soiled fabrics and stuffed them into the bags, lining the full bags up in the hallway outside the door. The room stank from the urine and once I'd finished salvaging what was left undamaged, I got a pan and thick dish gloves and scrubbed the room thoroughly. When that was done, I pulled my suitcases out from beneath the bed and began filling them with everything that hadn't been destroyed. Carrie's clothes went right in with my own. I took apart her crib, using plastic wire ties to lash the pieces together. From there I moved into the kitchen, once again washing and putting things away where they belonged and gathering garbage for the growing pile in the hallway. I looked at the sofa, but there was little I could do to salvage it. I ended up pulling a flat bed sheet from the linen closet and throwing it over the sofa like a cover, tucking it in around the cushions.

There wasn't much more I could do so I began my multiple trips down to the car and the dumpster until the apartment looked barren, but not so macabre.

I took the time to sit down and write a note to Bitsy on the inside of a flattened cereal box. I told her I was sorry, but that I had brought danger in on her in the person of Colt Stillman. I didn't go into detail, but she would see the sofa and know something had happened. I told her I was moving home again, that I was quitting my job. It was more likely my job had already quit me, but I didn't need to explain that. I told her that as soon as I found work, I would send money for my share of the rent through the end of the lease and if I could spare it, a little extra so that she could ride the bus down and visit me and Carrie. I knew she had become attached to my daughter and I couldn't just dump her that way. My closing words were to wish her well with Buddy and to beware of his friend. There was nothing left to say, so I scribbled my signature and wedged the cardboard into the edge of the cupboard door where she was sure to see it. I wasn't sure what to do about the broken lock, so I went back inside and added a postscript to the note, telling her to have it fixed and to bill me for it. It was all I could do under the circumstances.

I needed to leave town and not waste time. Colt had more than likely read the look on my face. I wasn't safe. The man had money, connections and he was not stupid. I had nowhere else to go, but home.

With Carrie in the car seat and our belongings, or what was left of them, stowed in the trunk, we left the Chicago skyline in the rearview mirror. I felt the crushing disappointment that my dreams had failed.

Metallica had been curt, and I don't think very surprised. In fact, I had probably saved her the trouble of firing me. It wasn't so much that I'd lost control of the meeting, as it was that I'd withheld the information about Carrie. I suspected Metallica was not the motherly type and had hoped to see me as a career woman who would settle for nothing less. I would never give up my daughter, but I had to admit that solitude looked pretty good about then.

Goodbye Chicago. Goodbye Colt Stillman.

Chapter 17

Coulter

It was three weeks following Buddy's accident and we were moving him into the best physical therapy complex I could find. Every patient was given a personal workup and the therapist to patient ratio was one to three. In between workouts, Buddy was served five-star meals and given massages by the industry's best. I saw to it that he didn't need to worry about a thing. Luckily, the surgery had worked and once the swelling reduced, Buddy regained consciousness on his own. Other than the physical therapy needed to regenerate his body strength and flexibility, he had come through it like a champ. He was strong and as I reminded him, I'd never had any doubt.

My commitment to my friend also required that I look after his business interests until he could return. It added considerably to my workload but I was more than willing to do it. I had no life of my own any longer, not since Gwen left.

Bitsy was probably the most loyal person I'd ever encountered. Not only was she there each and every day for Buddy, but she protected Gwen furiously and wouldn't tell me a thing. While I was fairly sure Gwen had gone back to her family, what left me baffled was the reason why. We'd spent that wonderful evening together and I had felt the beginning of something new rising in my chest. It involved pride, a sense of belonging, and yes, love. Then came the accident and everything changed.

I was breathing, there was no better way to describe it. I had opened my heart and trusted and for some reason, she turned her back on me and left, again. I spent long hours and many bourbons debating whether I should go after her. For the immediate future, it was out of the question. I was too busy with Buddy and his obligations. Then I had my own businesses to look after. All my permits had been restored and the busiest season for building was upon us. Whatever was wrong with Gwen, she needed to sort it out for herself. She needed to put some time and space between us. God, but I wish I knew what had her so terrorized. She didn't trust me, that much was evident.

So, it was early winter, and Buddy was finally to the point where he could put a couple hours into work each day and was becoming stronger. He said they told him he would be himself again within a year, to just add to his duties gradually. He asked Bitsy to move in with him once he was able to go back to his condo. She hadn't hesitated, and I didn't blame her. Not only was he, in my opinion, one of the greatest guys on the planet, he needed her and she responded to that. I sent a couple of guys with her to the apartment to clear out her things, but they'd returned with an empty truck. She'd told them it wasn't necessary, she was leaving almost everything behind in the dumpster. I guessed

Buddy was her future and I wished them both success and good health.

That left me with Gwen. Over the interim months, I'd gone through a series of phases. At first, I had been puzzled by her disappearance. Bitsy was not forthcoming and there was no other explanation as far as I could find. I even sent my receptionist back to the dress shop and she asked for Gwen by name but was told that she no longer worked there and could someone else help her. It was a dead end.

Gwen had never picked up the car I bought her. I probably hadn't handled that well. I should have given it to her face to face, but with Buddy's accident, well, there just wasn't an opportunity. I felt compelled to look after her and her child. Giving her safe transportation was a very small part of what I was willing to do.

The next phase I went through was anger. I asked myself what I had done to alienate her? Had I not been a good lover, or had I been too good? Had I reminded her of someone and was that someone the person who rooted the distrust in her? Had I ignored her? No, I didn't think so. If anything, I had pursued her beyond the normal fashion. Maybe that was it. Maybe I didn't give her the space she needed. Whatever it was, she was gone and that's when I moved into the final phase.

I missed her. There was no simpler way of stating it. I

was in love with the woman and the woman wanted nothing to do with me. Life became colorless for me. There was no longer any challenge in building a skyscraper or fighting with the unions. Money had never been an issue so making more seemed redundant. My parents could see the change in my attitude and asked me about it over long dinners at their house on weekends. I started going there more frequently than I had before, simply because it gave me a sense of belonging. I became the little boy who was homesick, how silly was that?

I tried dating other women. It didn't work. They didn't have her hair, her eyes, her mouth or that sweet, voluptuous body that had nestled against my back the night we spent together. I rejected each one in turn, almost to the point of cruelty before I finally called it quits and accepted the fact that there was no other woman who would ever make me happy again.

That left me with one choice. I had to find her, and I had to win her back. The finding part wasn't hard. I put my guy on it and a couple of hours later, I had an address and phone number. I knew where she was. I told Peter to pack a bag and sent to him down to Brookfield. His job was to lay low but watch high, in a matter of speaking. He was my man on the ground and he reported to me at least six times a day. He found her but she was not aware of it. He made several inquiries in town and just as I had thought, there had been a man early on who was Carrie's father. He had joined the

Army and at some point, the Army decided they no longer wanted him. How that affected her, I wasn't sure, but I wanted to be certain she was safe. That, too, for the meantime, was Peter's job.

I had him scout out a location for a new business. I had no great thirst for starting yet another company, but I wanted a reason to move to Brookfield and to do my own watching. He found a manufacturing company that was on the edge of foreclosure. They produced health and beauty aids for generic brand labeling. The company should have expanded long before and that lack of foresight had led to the competition swallowing them. They held a few patents, which was a plus, but their equipment was antiquated and slow. Their employees were underpaid and frequently injured. In the normal course of things, they would have gone out of business through mere attrition. In my usual style, I was going to interfere with that. Thus, I bought Marshall Manufacturing.

I rented a car and wore sunglasses and a ball cap to disguise my appearance. I went by the name of Mr. Marshall, with Tom as my first name. The employees were told I was a cousin of the original founder and they accepted that without question. They were only too happy that I had become involved because it meant that their jobs were safe. I closed up my condo and moved to Brookfield, purchasing a large rustic cabin deep in the woods not far from the company. I had privacy fencing with security installed on the perimeter and for all purposes, became a hermit except for the time I spent at the factory. I was always in disguise, with only Peter knowing who I really was. I'd hired someone to take my place in the city until such time as Buddy was back up to full speed and would take over for me. I'd already decided to stay in Brookfield permanently.

I had a small staff at the cabin, people I brought with me who weren't interested in local gossip. There was a housekeeper, a groundskeeper, a security man, and Peter lived in a guest cottage at the edge of the property. It seemed he had, in the course of investigating for me, met a young local girl and become quite enamored. He never let it interfere with his job and I allowed him to bring her onto the estate to stay with him at the cottage from time to time. It was a situation that seemed to meet everyone's needs. Everyone, but me.

I revamped the entire plant, installing state-of-the-art equipment, instated the latest in production techniques, and gave salary increases with benefits including an on-site health club, restaurant, daycare, and a few shops. In many ways, working for me was better than living in town. I kept quality high and the prices dirt low. There was a waiting list for jobs as they opened up.

As much as I wanted to, I didn't try to see Gwen. There was too great a chance she would see through my disguise and that would ruin everything. Once the plant was running smoothly, I put a supervisor in charge and retreated to the cabin. I sent Peter out to make sure that Gwen needed a job and was hired at Marshall Manufacturing. She was given an administrative job, one that gave her some managerial control. I thought that might help her to restore a bit of the insecurity she built since that first relationship. Word got back to me that she was doing well, in fact, she was very good at her job. She was well-paid, far above that of the others and for that reason, anyone who divulged their salary was instantly fired. I watched her now that I was on high. I watched her, and I waited for my chance.

Chapter 18

Gwen

Carrie and I were living with my parents in the sleepy town of Brookfield once again. It says somewhere that all roads lead back home again and I guess in my case, that was true. Carrie loved it. She thrived with the added attention that my parents lavished on her. Their house was large enough that we had separate rooms and Carrie began to walk if what somewhat unsteadily. Her room was filled with toys, the bounty she gained from my parents, my friends, and myself. Babies were like that. It made people feel better to see a baby play; maybe it was reliving their own childhood. There was no lack of babysitters, including my old friend, Patsy. She'd appeared on the horizon from the beginning, listening to my tales of woe and encouraging me that now that I was home again, things would work out okay.

I found a job at the local grocery store as a cashier. I was certainly overqualified but very grateful to have the job, so I made the best of it. My feet were a little sore at first, the long hours standing there, scanning people's purchases. But as it turned out, it was a good way to get reacquainted with the people I'd known and missed. They told me their aches and pains, their griefs, and broken hearts. I could relate. My own heart was broken. I still couldn't figure out what had turned Colt into the man who had destroyed my apartment in such a malicious, pointed way.

There were still phone calls to my parents' house which when I answered, there were a few moments of breathing and then the line disconnected. There was no number to trace and no way to block it from a landline. I was stuck with it and suggested to my parents that they invest in cell phones and get rid of the landline entirely. Mom was rather excited by the idea, but dad, being a banker, saw no savings in changing. He'd done things the same way for a hundred years and he would continue for the next hundred. I couldn't blame him. There was a certain amount of security in doing things the same way.

My car had held up pretty well for its age. There were days when it wasn't quite as cooperative, and I had to walk to work. It didn't bother me. Even though it was cold, the air was refreshing, and it was good exercise. Dad always offered to drive me, but I refused. I didn't want to become dependent on anyone, not even my own father.

Mom and Dad had plans to go to their timeshare in Florida for the coldest part of the winter. They would be leaving right after Christmas. They had done this the past five years, but this year I would miss them especially. Carrie and I would have the house to ourselves, but somehow that felt a little spooky.

The mysterious phone calls continued. I knew they must be Colt. Only he had the persistence to carry it off. I missed him, I won't lie. Even though he had been intrusive to the point of irrational, I had gotten a little used to it and that evening we had spent together was the best of my life. I don't know what turned him that next morning and made him behave as he did. Perhaps I would never find out. It was one of those things I was dying to know, but afraid to find out.

Mom and Dad had left for Florida and Carrie and I moved to their downstairs bedroom. It helped to make things feel a little cozier in the big empty house. My job at the grocery store was becoming unbelievably boring, and it was only the thought of going home that kept the light at the end of the tunnel. I kept in touch with my friends and from time to time would ask one or two of the girls to come over and spend the night. We talked about old days and the boys we had known. One of the girls told me about job openings at the newly acquired Marshall Manufacturing. While I really wasn't interested in assembly line work, there was an outside chance that there might be an opening in their executive offices. I played around with the idea of applying but didn't act on it. One day, a young man came through the grocery line. He looked out of place, wearing an expensive topcoat and leather gloves. No one in Brookfield dressed like that, especially to go only to the grocery store. He was nice, good-looking, and very conversational.

I hadn't noticed him speaking to anyone else as he waited in line, but when he reached me, he couldn't seem to stop talking. I thought that was rather odd, except for the fact that he was dressed like an out-of-towner and couldn't understand how things operated. I could see he was rather uncomfortable, so I engaged in discussion, hoping to make him relax a little.

"So, you don't look like you're from around here," I began.

"No, you're right, I'm not."

"Maybe from Chicago?"

"Could be, something like that. You look familiar to me," he said.

"Really? Well, you're not from around here, I grew up here. Of course, there was a short stint when I lived in Chicago."

“What do you know. Maybe that’s where I saw you. You just looked so familiar to me."

“So, what brings you to Brookfield?" I was dragging out the discussion as long as I could. Oddly enough, he was buying 50 or so bottles of water, not in one handy pack, but in separate, individual bottles. I should've just counted them and multiplied that by one ring through, but we were having a conversation and it seemed sort of natural.

"Oh, just business."

"Oh?"

"Yeah. I'm with the new manufacturing company. Well, it's not exactly new, but I got hired on as an assistant to the new manager."

“Wow, that's great for you. "

"Actually, you look and sound kind of overqualified to work here at the grocery store. Have you thought about putting an application with Marshall?"

"No, not really. I'm really not much of a line person." We both laughed as we realized he was in my line.

"Well, hey, you know, there are jobs in the offices. Maybe one of those would suit you better?"

He was looking at me directly and while he was being attentive, there was something odd about it. I knew I had become overly suspicious, especially since Mom and Dad left Florida, leaving Carrie and I to ourselves. "You know, I might just give them a call and see what's available."

“Oh, hey, that would be great. Tell you what," he said, reaching into his pocket and pulling on his business card, handing it in my direction. "Tell them I sent you and tell them I said to treat you right."

I laughed, accepting the card and sliding it into my

jeans pocket. "I might just do that, don't be surprised if you see me around."

I thought about that man all afternoon as I worked. In fact, the more I thought about having a job that was less on my feet and took a little more brainpower, the harder my job as a cashier became. By the time I clocked out, I've made up my mind to try Marshall Manufacturing. After all, what did I have to lose?

* * *

The man across the desk from me held out his hand to shake. "Thank you very much for coming in, Gwen. Here is a packet of papers for you to complete, and we look forward to seeing you here on Monday. You did say that childcare would not be a problem, correct?"

"I did say that. And it won't be. Although, I think you weren't supposed to ask me that."

The man looked surprised, even embarrassed. I wondered if he was doing his job or had boned up on all the discrimination laws when it came to hiring people. I let it go, though, because it meant that I had a brand-new job Monday morning. As a matter of fact, I was going to be the assistant to Peter, the young man who had come through my checkout lane. I thought that not only ironic, rather fun. I thought we would get along well. Of course, I would have to teach him how to dress, but I figured he was a quick learner. Yes, he was going to be an interesting experience.

I picked up Carrie from the daycare on my way home. As usual, she burst into a big grin as she saw me, and as usual, I hugged and kissed her until I thought I couldn't stop. We had become very close, she and I, even though she only had a vocabulary of about twenty words which included “cookie, cereal, mama, grandma, grandpa."

It hurt me that there was no “dad," included, but the rest of us made up for what she may have missed not having him.

Carrie and I arrived back at my parents' house. There was an envelope; the large, business kind, stuffed into the mailbox. It was so large they'd been unable to shut the mailbox door. I put Carrie on my hip and grappled with the envelope to get it out. There was no return address and the addressee was me and it was handwritten. I thought that was unusual and wondered who might be sending me a package. It wasn't as if I didn't live right there in town.

We got inside, and I put Carrie in her playpen as I sat down with the bulky envelope. I questioned whether I should open something when I knew nothing about who sent it. The small town in me, trusting everyone said otherwise, so I went ahead. Inside I found hundreds of newspaper pages which had all been run through a shredder. This I found puzzling and dumped them all out in a pile on the floor. I sorted through a few, trying to find some puzzle matches so that I might understand if the stuffing was the purpose of the envelope, or whether there was something that had been merely cushioned by it in there.

I could finally tell they were pages from the local newspaper here in Brookfield. I found the date on one; it was two years previous. Beyond that, it was impossible to gather anything that was recognizable. The newspaper was brittle, which told me that it was all old, something I found more than a little creepy. I bundled it all together, stuffed it back into the envelope and threw it into the trash can in the driveway. I didn't even want it in the house.

Once I got back into the house, Carrie was crying and the whole experience was very unnerving. I had no idea why someone would send me an envelope full of shredded newspaper clippings. Apparently, they had some sort of significance to whoever set them, but I had no clue. Was this another act, was it his way of telling me that he was watching me? Could he be this sick?

I found that thought frightening and wished my parents weren't in Florida. There was no one to look out for me and no one to look after Carrie if something happened to me. I just didn't know what I was dealing with. It was all so uncertain. After dinner that night, I put Carrie to bed early. I sat for a long time in the front room looking out the window and going through the suspects in my mind once again. The more I thought, the more panicked I became and the bigger the house felt. I scrambled for my phone and tapped Patsy's number.

"Patsy, I'm going to ask you something rather silly, but please, help me out if you can. Could you come? Could you come and stay with Carrie and me for a while?"

"Well, I guess I could. Why? What's wrong?"

"I don't want to go into the whole story right now. But something came in the mail today and it really freaked me out. It worries me."

"No problem. I love that big old house. And it would be a treat to come stay with you. It would be just like old times."

"Good. Then I'll expect to see you soon."

"I'll be there."

Chapter 19

Coulter

"Did you give her the job?" I asked Peter. We were sitting in Adirondack chairs on the expansive front porch of my cabin.

"Just as you asked," Peter responded, taking a sip of his beer. Although it was still early Spring, the day was unusually warm and we both needed the fresh scent of air to clear our heads.

"And did she seem like she was happy?" I wanted to know every nuance, every detail.

"Yes, she did. Actually, she's really sweet, if you don't mind my saying so. At the grocery store, she took time to talk with me and process all those bottles of water."

"I figured those would set her off."

"No, not at all. Like I said, she was really nice. When she applied and found out she'd be my assistant, it seemed to surprise her pleasantly."

"Pay attention to what I tell you to do. The last thing I want her to do is to quit and run off again. I'm in this thing deep this time."

"I understand, boss."

"Tom Marshall."

"Yes, sir, Mr. Marshall."

"God, don't slip up on that. It will kill everything."

Peter nodded.

"Did you take care of that other detail?"

"Yes, I did. All taken care of."

"Good."

"Mr. Marshall?"

"Yeah?"

"May I ask you a personal question?"

"Go ahead."

"Just exactly what are your intentions with her?"

"If it's any of your business, I'm going to make her my wife."

Chapter 20

Gwen

Working with Peter was probably the best job I've ever had. It was almost as if he was working for me. I had an office the same size as his and we left the door between us open. In the mornings, we lingered over repeated cups of coffee and gossiped about everyone and everything we could think of. He laughed at my jokes and made me feel clever and beautiful again. He was very good for my self-esteem.

I teased him about his girlfriend, Kathy, a lovely petite girl who worked for Marshall and seem to adore him. I saw his face light up every time she stopped by on some made-up pretense, just to see him. In some ways, though, it made me a little sad to think that I would never have that kind of new love again. I'd been burned twice and was in no hurry to repeat those mistakes again. I had my daughter, a good job, both my parents and lots of friends. What else did I need?

Secretly, though, I knew. The only problem was what I didn't know who he really was as a man. Was he the kind, caring, loving person who had held me in his arms that night, or did his need to control overstep everything in his path? I wish I knew because I missed him.

It was a beautiful day and I opened my windows to the outdoors. Peter stuck his head through the doorway and motioned to me. "Come with me, I have something to show you."

"Sure. What is it?"

"You'll find out shortly." I followed him as we left the building, women's eyes all around us trained on his back. I had to admit, I understood their lust. He was young, very good-looking, affable, brilliant, and liable to be a major player someday. If I hadn't already had that aching love in my heart, I might've been interested, too.

He went to the exit door and held it open for me. I wasn't sure what he was going to show me but was glad the weather was warm because I'd left my jacket inside. We walked out into the parking lot. I was puzzled. "Are we going somewhere?"

"No, not me, anyway."

My heart sank. I realized then what was going on.

I was being fired.

He hadn't told me inside because company policy held that people being fired were walked out of the building before they were told. It prevented scenes. Any moment now, someone would come out with my purse, my jacket, and my picture of Carrie from my desk. I would be told that I was no longer needed, but I would receive two weeks' pay as severance and I could continue on the company health plan as long as I paid my own premium. I'd seen it happen so many times before, particularly with the former owner of that very company. I felt the tears began to well up in my eyes and that sick feeling crept into my stomach.

What was I going to do? I couldn't live off my parents. I had quit the job at the grocery store and been so happy to do it; more than likely I'd burned any bridges there were. It was a small town and there weren't many jobs to be had. I didn't even have a degree.

I was so busy counting my woes that I overlooked Peter, his hand pointing over my shoulder. "Turn around."

I froze. *Were they going to frisk me?* Did they think I was sneaking out the tape dispenser? "Peter, just break it to me, would you? Haven't we become good enough friends that you could take a little pity and just get it over quickly?"

His eyebrows rose, and he cocked his head. "Gwen, what the hell are you talking about?"

"Well, isn't this how it's done?"

"How what is done?"

"Aren't I being fired?"

"Aren't you being... where did you get that idea? If this company were to shut down, you would be the last one out of the door. Hell, I'd get fired before you would."

I thought that was an odd comment, but my relief caused me to overlook it. "Then, what is it?"

"Would you just turn around and look?"

I turned around and the most obvious thing was a soft blue, Cadillac SUV. It sat before me like a trophy, wearing a huge white bow on its roof. "Did you get a new car?"

"Did I… My God, Gwen. You are the hardest person I know to surprise. Hasn't anyone ever done anything good for you?"

"Me? Are you saying that's for me?"

"Of course, who else?"

"Now, wait a minute. I don't see any other baby blue Cadillacs around here. Why am I getting one?"

"Well, in the first place, you've been doing a marvelous job and I talked you up to the boss. He said he'd like to reward your hard work and that you would be a very good liaison between him and the rest of the people in the company. He's not from around here, you know, and he thinks that it would be very helpful if you could let him know when there are problems in the plant or any personal issues with the employees. He wants everyone to be happy and things to run smoothly and feels as though they don't all trust him yet."

"And for that, I get a Cadillac?"

He nodded. "Yes, and no. Yes, you are getting the Cadillac, but no it's not just because the boss wants to reward you. You will also be asked to run an errand from time to time between here and the boss' house or to pick up someone from the bus station, or the airport, or whatever. You know. Consider it like a company car except that it belongs to you."

"Peter! I can't even afford to pay the taxes on that thing or put gasoline in it. No, thank you. I'll keep my little beater."

"Sorry. I can't do that. The boss was very firm on this. He told me if you refused, that I was fired. You don't want me to be fired, do you? Anyway, here's a company credit card. Your insurance, gasoline, maintenance, everything gets charged to that card. It's not going to cost you a penny and it won't show up on your W-2." He held out a key ring and grinned. "Here you go. Why don't you take it for a ride?"

I was shaking my head, still confused. "Peter, this isn't normal. I've only been here a few weeks. There are people working here for gosh, more than thirty years. Their whole lives some of them. Why should I get a car and they don't?"

"Don't worry about them. The boss takes care of everyone in one way or another. This is what he wants to do for you, and like I said, my job depends on it and you will be using it for company business. So, please, can you just take it for a drive, tell me how much you love it and let me tell the boss that my job is safe?"

I was out of arguments, which was rare. I took the keys from his hand and walked over to the Cadillac, running my hand over the dove-blue paint job. "I think this is the most beautiful thing I've ever seen."

"They tell me it's pretty good in winter, too. That should keep you and Carrie safe."

There was something about his words that sounded familiar, but again, I was ecstatically happy and not paying attention. I opened the door and looked inside. The interior was a creamy white tufted leather and matching carpet. I carefully climbed into it, tapping my shoes on the doorframe in case there was any sand on my soles. I slid the key into the ignition and turned it. It began humming with an underlying base that rocked my heart. This was the sexiest thing I'd ever sat in. I turned on the sound system and strains of Rachmaninoff's Rhapsody filled its interior. "Shoot, I'm just going to live in here."

Peter was laughing. "You don't know how much pleasure it gives me to see you so happy."

"Well, who wouldn't be? Oh, my God," I said, clapping my hand over my mouth.

"What's wrong?"

"What are people going to say? You and I are always laughing and neither one of us do very much work. When they find out I got a company car like this, oh my God, they're going to think we're sleeping together."

"As delightful of a thought as that may be, my dear Gwen, we are not and do not intend to and I give you my word on that. So, to hell with what they think, enjoy your new car. Take the rest of the day off. Go pick up your daughter and ride the country roads with the windows open. It's too beautiful of a day to let it pass."

"Peter?"

"Yes?"

"I think I love you."

"I'm sure you do," he said, laughing as he walked back into the building and left me with my new toy.

Chapter 21

Coulter

"So? Did she like it?"

"Yes, Mr. Marshall, I would say that was an understatement. Of course, she went through all the arguments you anticipated. She was suspicious, she was afraid the others would talk and think that she and I were having an affair, she was afraid she couldn't pay the taxes, gas, or insurance, and of course, I assured her none of those were worth worrying about."

"Did you give her the card?"

"Yes, sir, I certainly did."

"Good. I bet she looked great in it."

"If you don't mind my saying so, sir, she would look great in anything, but baby blue and cream leather certainly are her style."

"Good. Now, here's what's next. I've watched the weather report and the supposed to stay warm, at least enough to be outside. A week from Saturday, I'm going to host a company picnic. I want you to line up the works. Bring in tents, plenty of seating, games for the kids, pony rides, a dance floor and music, and for God sakes, lots of beer and delicious food."

Peter raised his eyebrows. "And we are celebrating...?"

"Do we need to celebrate anything?"

"Well, if I'm going to spread the invitation, they're probably going to want to know why they should come."

"Good thinking. Tell them I want to thank them for sticking with the company through the transition. Tell them I want them to get to know me and what life will be like at Marshall manufacturing from here on out. I want to earn their loyalty, I want to benefit the community, and between you and me, I want to make Gwen happy. Taking care of her friends and family will do that."

"She is one lucky lady." Peter finished making his notes and stood to leave.

"Oh, and Peter?"

"Sir?"

"It's me who's lucky."

Chapter 22

Gwen

I had Carrie dressed in an adorable little outfit with blue jeans and a checked shirt. She was wearing a hand-knitted, navy sweater and baby-sized capital Keds tennis shoes. She could totter along on her own very well, but I held her hand on the uneven ground at the estate.

Mr. Marshall had invited the entire company's employees and their families to a picnic. Peter told me what a generous and kind man he was and that he wanted everyone to be happy that they stuck it out through the transition. The weather was perfect and as Carrie and I parked and began our walk toward the massive log home; I felt like we had entered one of Disney's Wonderlands.

There was an entire children's carnival set up to one side. There were ponies to ride, little colored cars on the merry-go-round, games where you could win prizes, and an entire table set up with plain cupcakes and dozens of colors of frosting and various toppings. The kids were going crazy over that. They could make up anything they wanted and eat to their hearts' delight. I hoped secretly that Mr. Marshall had good dental insurance because there were a lot of cavities in the making that day. I let Carrie make one cupcake, but most of it ended up on her face before it made it inside her mouth. I cheered her on and wiped her with a napkin and continued on.

There was a staff set aside to watch the children, so the adults could circulate and eat at will. The entire affair was so very thoughtful, and I knew everyone appreciated it. Everywhere I went, I heard Mr. Marshall's name bandied about. People were enamored of him and the word was that there was a list hundreds of names deep of people waiting to apply for an opening. I didn't think there were going to be many coming up very soon, and I was very glad that I had met Peter and ended up his assistant.

Patsy had moved in with us and while she made me feel a little safer, she was another version of Bitsy. There were some things that just escaped her. She helped to look after Carrie when I went to run errands and that helped a lot. Still, odd little things happened from time to time. They weren't really destructive—things like my garbage can was brought back up to the side of the house before I got home. No one in the neighborhood would do that. That meant someone who didn't belong there had done it for me. Then there were the pizza deliveries, every Friday night. The delivery boy wouldn't say who'd ordered them, but they were always prepaid and had the exact toppings I loved. I told the boy not to bring any more, but he said he had his orders and they would just rot on the front porch if I didn't take them in.

Then there was the matter of a wardrobe. Peter greeted me one morning after the car and handed me a credit card with my name on it. “The boss says you’re to go out and buy yourself a wardrobe,” he told me.

“Why?”

“For the same reason that you got the Cadillac. He wants you to represent the company well and feels that it would be an undue financial burden on you, so he’d like you to treat yourself to whatever you want and just use that card. Don’t worry, there’s no limit to it.”

I just stood there with the card in my hand and my mouth hanging open. There had to be more to it than that. Why was that man showering me with these gifts? Was it really and truly just part of the job?

That was one reason that I went to the picnic that day. I wanted to thank him personally for all he’d done for the community. I also needed to thank him for what he had done for me. It was almost as if he knew exactly what I needed, which was impossible because I’d never even seen the man, much less met him. In fact, there was a lot of speculation as to who he was. Some people said he was in his late 50s, short, fat, and bald. They said his wife had left him for a guy who owned a McDonald’s and that his heart had been broken. I thought that sounded a little hokey, but there were other rumors.

Some people said he was an invalid, a man who had made a lot of money in his life and now, just as he was dying, he decided to become benevolent and adopted the company and the local townspeople as his pseudo-family. They said he wanted someone to show up for his funeral when he died. Now that version seemed a little more plausible to me, but then, there was nothing for sure.

I found Peter who, as usual, was overdressed in a navy suit with a pinstripe shirt and red tie.

"You look like you're ready for Fourth of July," I teased him, and he had the good grace to blush.

"Is it really that bad?"

I nodded and leaned forward to pinch his arm. "Just teasing. Listen, Peter, I'd like the opportunity to meet Mr. Marshall. He has done a lot for me and for this community and I would like to represent all of us and tell him thank you. Is he inside?"

Peter looked over his shoulder and then back at me. "Yes, he's inside, but he won't come out until he's ready. He's like that, very private."

"Well, how do I go about making an appointment with him?"

"Don't worry. He knows you're here. You'll see him

eventually." Peter was very enigmatic in his statement and wandered away before I could ask any more questions. That didn't escape my notice.

There was a professional party organizer on hand. She was hired in from Chicago, someone said, and she got up on a stage with a microphone and announced that there was going to be a play. She had scripts for a dozen people, costumes, and was looking for volunteers for the parts. A number of hands went up and she chose people appropriately. She pointed at me.

"You, I want you to play the female lead."

"Me? No, I'm not an actress."

"Doesn't matter," she said, shaking her head, and motioning me up on the stage. Everyone around us began to applaud and I had no choice but to mount the stage steps and take the script she was holding out to me.

She rounded up some of the people to assemble a pre-painted backdrop for the stage. The rest of us were sent to tents to be costumed. We were expected to memorize our lines but held our scripts for guidance. It was a spoof on Shakespeare's *Romeo and Juliet* and guess who was Juliet.

Carrie was safely in the hands of the daycare workers but was given a front row seat when I emerged from backstage in my Juliet costume. I had to admit, it was almost as if it had been made for me. The gown matched my eye color perfectly and my long, blonde hair was braided down my back. A tiara was settled upon my head, as though I was a princess, which Juliet was not.

I went through the motions and waited to see who Romeo would be. Imagine my surprise when Romeo's first lines came up and Peter emerged from stage left, carrying a chimpanzee wearing tights and a beaded tunic. He held the animal as if it were speaking the lines, but he was the ventriloquist behind. It was hysterical. When he spoke the lines to challenge Mercutio in the sword fight, the chimp was given a paper sword and waved it furiously through the air. The man who played Mercutio was laughing so hard, he fell to his knees and the entire effect was perfect. It was a shortened version, thank God, because people were laughing so hard they couldn't speak, eat, or drink. It was the most perfect afternoon.

People were beginning to leave when Peter came up to me. "He wants to see you now."

"Now?" I was still wearing my Juliet costume.

"Yes, right now. Don't bother to change. I'll take care of Carrie."

"But where?"

He pointed out to the cabin. "Go in the front door, up

the staircase and it's the second door on the right. That's his home office. No need to knock, just walk in.

I wondered at all the mystery involved, it made me feel a little uncomfortable.

Chapter 23

Coulter

I heard her coming up the stairs, although her footsteps were light. I had my ear pressed to the door and as she came close, I vaulted over my desk like a twelve-year-old and sat there, waiting. I'd only seen her from afar since she'd left Chicago. I felt my heart pounding and my groin ached with wanting her.

The door opened and there she was. My Juliet.

"You." Her word was more of an accusation than a realization.

I nodded. "Yes, me."

She rolled her eyes and threw her arms out to her side. "How could I not know this?"

I shrugged. "I went to a great deal of trouble to make sure you wouldn't."

"Why?"

"Because you would run again."

"But..."

"Well? You would have, wouldn't you? You wouldn't have taken the job, or the car or the expense account. You wouldn't have taken anything that came from me, even if you'd earned it. Am I right?"

She nodded resignedly. "You're right. Why, Colt? Why do you continue to pursue me? Why did you do all that you did?"

"I'm in love with you."

She sucked in her breath and went pale. I came around the desk, walked her to the leather sofa and handed her a snifter filled with brandy. Getting one for myself, I sat down next to her.

"You have a lot of explaining to do."

"Ask away."

"Why did you destroy my apartment. All my things? My wardrobe, for heaven's sake, Colt. I'm still paying for it and never got to wear a fraction of it. Why would you do that to me?"

What was she talking about? "Gwen, you have to believe me. I don't know what you're talking about. Who broke into your apartment and when was this?"

"It wasn't you?"

"Hell, no! Why would I do something like that? That's insane!"

She looked at the snifter and nodded. "Now that you put it like that, I see your point. But there wasn't anyone else, Colt. Everyone else was accounted for."

"It could have been some kid, looking for dope money. God, Gwen, I don't know."

"No, this was deliberately aimed at me. Bitsy and Carrie's things were untouched. Mine were destroyed."

I felt alarm and anger surfacing. "Who would hate you that much?"

She shook her head. "No one I can think of. No one, Colt. I thought you were trying to control me—that you ruined my things so I would be forced to take what you gave me. I thought that's why it was only my stuff that was destroyed."

"Jesus, Gwen, does that sound like me?" I rolled my eyes. "Do you really consider me a maniac?"

She shook her head.

I went to hold her, but she held me off. "What about the phone calls with no answer? The envelope of shredded newspapers? The pizzas?"

I was really getting alarmed then. "Gwen, listen to me. I send pizzas to your house because I know you're tired on Friday nights and I wanted you to relax. But that's it. I know nothing about phone calls or shredded newspaper. You have to tell me who would have reason to do this to you."

"That's it—I don't know. I blamed you only because I couldn't think of anyone else. I'm sorry."

"Well, that's flattering."

"Colt, don't be like that," she said, reaching out to me. "I was scared. Everything was weird, and the apartment thing felt really invasive. You have to admit you've been following me. You know I asked you not to."

I had to admit it. "Yes, that's true. I'm not wanting to spook you, Gwen. God, no. That's the last thing. I'm in love with you and don't want to lose you. The rest, well, I am trying to take care of you."

"All I want is someone to trust, Colt. That's it."

I felt cold inside as I stared at the wreckage that was the woman I loved. "It was him that made you this way, wasn't it? Carrie's father."

She froze and then began to cry, nodding. I handed her tissues and held her. I wanted her to get it all out.

"I'm not going to ask you about it because that's your past. You are my future. I want you to marry me, Gwen. Come here and live with me, you and Carrie. We'll stay here in Brookfield—hell, I'm sort of starting to like the little place. Let me look after the both of you. I don't need to work, except if I get bored and somehow I don't think life around you could be boring."

"Yes."

"Yes?"

"Yes."

"Yes, what?"

"Yes, I will marry you."

"Oh, my god, Gwen, you're not even going to put up an argument? I love you, and I don't want to question this, but what turned you around? A moment ago, you came in here accusing me of vandalism, terrorism and I don't know what else. What changed your mind?"

"Because, I love you, too. I knew it the moment I walked in here and saw you. It was like we'd never been apart. I've missed you so much and even though I thought those horrible things about you, it never made me stop loving you. I figure that's a good start to get through a marriage."

I pulled her against me and hugged her so tightly she began pounding my back to release her. "Can't... breathe..." she gasped, and I kissed her.

"Let me give you a little mouth-to-mouth."

She nodded, but I reached over and lifted her up, against me and took her down the hall to my bedroom.

"My sweet Juliet. I had the costume made for you especially."

"I thought the colors were a perfect match," she smiled.

I set her down and reached behind her and began unbraiding her hair, laying the tiara on the nightstand. "I want to see you naked," I whispered, and she nodded and began removing her clothes.

When she finally stood before me in all her glory, I couldn't imagine anything more beautiful. She came toward me and began unbuttoning my shirt, pulling the tail out of my pants and then undid my belt. A few, swift hand movements and my clothes were in a puddle on the floor with her gown. We stood naked against one another, man against woman.

I reached forward and touched her breast, weighing it in my hands. "Have I told you how beautiful you are?"

"You can tell me again," she allowed.

"You are beautiful, my sweet Gwennie. I've been waiting for you all my life without knowing it. Since the moment I met you, you've been like a tune in my head I can't forget. I try to put you out of my mind, but you're always there."

I pushed her smoothly against the comforter and pushed her legs wide. I took her then, without preamble, without preparation, and without guilt. She had been mine for so long, I just wanted to finally claim her. I think she knew that because she became instantly pliable, receiving my thrusts and matching me, rhythm to rhythm.

There was a sweetness to our lovemaking. It was not sexual teasing or dominating roughness. We were reuniting what shouldn't have ever been separated—a recombination of spirits. We let our bodies celebrate the feel of one another, taking our time and letting skin excite skin. At one point, I stopped and pulled her hard against me. "Swear to me you won't leave again," I ordered her.

"I swear."

"Never?"

"Never, ever."

I thrust hard then, finding her depth and driving into

her with all the frustration and longing I'd felt for her. She answered me with her body and soon, the crest was upon us and the liquid fire spread through our bodies. I held her against my chest, not wanting to let go because I feared she'd run off again.

We lay there a very long time. "I have to go," she said, her head popping up. "Carrie."

"All taken care of. She's staying with Peter and Kathy at the cottage here on the estate. She's fine."

She opened her mouth to argue, but I saw the decision to trust me come into her eyes. She nodded, laid her head back on my chest and drifted off to sleep.

Chapter 24

Gwen

There was a pounding noise and I pushed away the deep, dreamless sleep to find its source. I felt Colt move on the bed next to me. "What is it?" I rolled over to ask.

He sat up, pulling on his pants. I grabbed the blankets to cover myself and watched as he went to the door and opened it. There stood a man in uniform.

"Mr. Marshall, we need you to come with us. There's a fire at your factory. People are hurt. Come on."

Colt looked over his shoulder and bent to grab his shirt and socks. "Gwen, I'm going to need Peter to go with me. I'll send Kathy with Carrie up here to the house. You stay put, you hear?"

I nodded and watched him leave, my heart pounding in my chest. When the men were gone, I ran to the window, hoping I could see something, but the forest surrounding the house was too dense. I quickly dressed in some sweatpants and a sweatshirt I found in Colt's closet. I folded up the legs and sleeves, so I wouldn't trip and ran down the stairs. Just as I arrived at the front door, there was a knock and I opened it to find Kathy, holding Carrie in her arms. "Thank you, just give her to me," I told her.

I looked around to get my bearings and remembered I brought my purse into Colt's office. I quickly went up the stairs to retrieve them and came back down, still in my bare feet. "I can drop you at the cottage, but I'm going home," I told her.

"I'll be okay on my own," she said, and I swept past her and ran out into the yard to find my car. I put Carrie inside and carefully drove down the long drive but turned to the right, so I wouldn't pass the factory. I wanted away from it all. It was all coming back to me. Colt in the defendant's chair. Colt with that smirk on his face. Colt, with the logical explanation for everything. Had he bought Marshall Manufacturing so he could be near me, to control my life in the very town where I grew up? Now that he felt he had me, did he want to rid himself of the obligation? He thought he had me, that I would go anywhere with them. He wanted to take me back to Chicago, I just knew it. I wasn't going anywhere. I was home.

I put Carrie to bed at the house and told Patsy what was going on. She was shocked and wanted to go down to the company, but I told her to stay home and keep the lights off. I wanted away from it all, to not be involved. I'd gotten caught once again.

* * *

The fire marshal opened an investigation. He had

found a pile of boxes that looked suspicious among the rubble. Although people were injured, none were hurt too seriously and they were being cared for the local hospital. The town was all abuzz, especially when it was learned that Colt's name was not Tom Marshall, but Coulter Stillman. It surfaced that he was a multi-billionaire from Chicago who had tracked me back to my hometown. The more that was said, the further I withdrew. The accusations, the open-ended justifications—so easily created by such an intelligent man. I didn't know what to think. I loved Colt and wanted to stand by his side. But I had to know. I had to know.

Chapter 25

Coulter

The courthouse overflowed onto the lawns of the town square as the entire community gathered to "be the first to know" what happened in the courtroom. I walked through the throng with Mason and received a mixed response. Some, who were my employees, nodded respectfully, but that's as good as it got. Others, who were only gawkers, behaved like they'd come to enjoy a good hanging and growled and shouted names.

I didn't see her. I was distraught. She had run again.

It remained undetermined whether the fire was deliberately set at Marshall Manufacturing. Either way, the families of those injured had done their research and unearthed the details of my trial in Chicago. The prosecutor, seeing the opportunity to make a name for himself, filed charges in a group action against me to claim I was negligent. It was the fastest action Mason had ever seen—the court docket had been cleared in favor of the expected drama, especially in light of the upcoming election for the prosecutor and the judge.

"Might as well get it over with," advised Mason in my office the day after the court papers arrived. "These hicks have no idea what they're doing. There's not even been proof it was arson! But we have to respond and clean up later. You're as innocent as hell and the sooner that's out, the sooner you can get down to the business of rebuilding and putting those people back to work."

"I really don't care anymore," I told him. "I'd be better off in a cell somewhere. Hell, Mason, she's walked on me again."

"Look, Colt, you've got bigger things to worry about at the moment. She'll be there when this is all over. Trust."

"Hell! What kind of trust did she have in me?"

Our conversation turned there as Mason made a couple of calls while I sat in misery. I barely heard him as he told me he'd put some guys he knew on rooting out the background and details. I nodded as he patted me on the back on his way out the door. I couldn't remember being that low.

So, there I was, entering the courtroom, again, for something I'd had no part in. People with money were always targets and I sure as hell was living proof.

Chapter 26

Gwen

I was on the back patio with Carrie, watching her stack plastic blocks as she sat on a blanket in the sunshine. She was innocent and pure—she was who I wanted to be again. I felt dirty, as though I'd put myself in the crosshairs of community judgment again and was found guilty. Everyone seemed to know that Colt and I had a history, and now my reputation was also on trial.

I didn't answer his calls because there hadn't been any. I guess he'd finally gotten the message. I didn't want to see him; he couldn't be trusted. Either way, the phone remained silent and my heart was going down in a Titanic sort of way. All I could do was focus on positives, like my tiny daughter playing in the sunshine.

Patsy came bursting through the slider, out of breath. She grabbed a folding chair and dragged it close, facing me. "He's innocent," she whispered excitedly, looking over her shoulder at Carrie.

I leaned forward, my eyes wide. "What happened?"

She shook her head. "I don't know the details, I couldn't get a seat inside, but the word came out to everyone outside. There was no negligence because arson couldn't be disproven. Everyone says the prosecutor got ahead of himself and pointed fingers when there was no proof of guilt. It's over, Gwen. You can go back to him now."

I shook my head. "No, I can't. I doubt he'd have me. Oh, Patsy, I've screwed up everything. What happened? My life used to be so simple. I had a future and it all looked so bright."

"Well, you've got Carrie, haven't you? You wouldn't wish *her* away, would you?"

"Of course not, but Carrie aside, it all started on graduation night."

"Paul..." Patsy acknowledged, nodding.

"Exactly." In a lightning bolt of thought, I began doubting myself. Was it possible that it wasn't Colt after all? Was I fixating on him and overlooking someone else who would fit into the weird pattern of what was happening?

"Patsy, listen..."

"You sound still upset."

"Yeah, you better believe it. Look, I don't want to get into all of this, because I'm not really sure what I'm dealing with, but do you have any idea when Paul has been home from the service on leave?"

"On leave? No, not exactly, because he’s not in the Army anymore."

"What? Paul's not in the Army?"

"Oh no, I thought you knew that. He wasn't in there very long at all and they gave him a general discharge, I think they call it? I'm not sure what that means but it's not dishonorable and it's not honorable, either one. I guess he just didn't fit in or they didn't want him around. I don't know why. I think he's a hunk and I always have, but you knew that."

"Patsy, have you seen him around town?"

“Sure, all the time. I thought you'd seen him too. In fact, I guess I figured you were seeing him socially."

"Are you serious? Do you know what that man did to me?"

"Well, I'm not sure how to ask this, but isn't Paul Carrie's father?"

There it was. Small town America in one sentence. I thought I had hidden things so well. I thought I was clever and that my reputation would vanish any nasty gossip, but I was so wrong. My best friend at home knew and never let on. *What was I thinking?* “How long have you known?”

"Well, I guess since the beginning. As soon as I knew you were pregnant. Who else could it have been, except Paul? I thought that's the reason you went to Chicago. You wanted to get away from him."

"Oh, my God. Here I thought I knew what I was doing, and it seems that everyone else did, too. Well, do me a favor, if you should happen to run across him, don't tell him that I'm home."

"Oh, it's too late. He already knows."

"What do you mean?"

"He was the one that told me you'd come home. Not the other times, just this time. I guess he wanted me to know that he knew."

There was a chill creeping down my spine and I felt sick to my stomach.

Patsy's head popped up. "I hear the doorbell. You sit tight, I'll get it."

She was only gone a minute. When she came back, Colt was standing behind her. "Uh, Gwen, Mr. Stillman is here to see you. I asked him to wait out front, but... well, you see."

My head snapped to look up at him, towering over me

like a dark tower of rage, about to explode.

"Uh, I think Carrie needs to go to the park," Patsy hurriedly put in, her eyes darting between me and Colt's face. "We'll be back after a while... uh... or... whenever," she stuttered, gathering up Carrie and her blocks and hurrying inside.

Colt waited until we heard Patsy's car start up and back down the drive.

"Sit down," I told him, hoping to disarm the anger I saw there and also put him at my level so I didn't have to look up at him so sharply. I knew I was delaying the inevitable. I had to hand it to him; he was holding himself in check.

"I won't be here long," he said tersely, but after a moment seemed to reconsider as he took Patsy's chair, although moving it further from me first.

I knew I'd better get it over with. "I heard they threw the case out of court."

"You weren't there." His words were low and deadly.

Where did the love in his eyes go? This was a Colt I'd not seen before. I'd never seen anyone with that much anger in his eyes.

"No, you're right, I wasn't."

"You judged me guilty and ran away again, didn't you?"

I nodded. "Yes, I did. Colt, I was wrong. I..."

"Save it," he said coldly and looked away. "I'm leaving this afternoon and going back to Chicago. In a few days, I'm leaving the country—going to take the jet and keep going until you don't matter anymore. I may never get back."

"Colt, no!"

He ignored me and continued on. "I love you, Gwen, and for that reason alone, I'm going to forgive you. I know what's behind this and I thought I could shake it from you, but you won't stay put long enough to even give us a chance. Every opportunity you've had, you've passed judgment. Not because I was on trial, but because finding me guilty absolved you of your own."

His words slammed into my chest and mind with the force of a ragged sword. *He's right! Oh, my God, he's right.*

He saw his words hit home—read the realization on my face. He slapped his hands on his knees and leaned forward, preparing to stand and leave. "Buddy will be running my companies. You know how to reach him. If you ever, and I mean *ever* need anything, call him."

I couldn't help myself. "No credit limit on *that* card, huh?"

His face screwed up into a look of angry distaste. "Why would you say something so crude? That's not you, Gwen."

I began to cry. My shoulders shook as I began rocking back and forth in my seat. "No, no, it's not me, Colt. And it's never been you. You haven't done anything to ever hurt me. You've only been kind and generous—looking after me and my daughter. I don't deserve you, Colt. You're right. I do feel guilty. I let my guard down and I got pregnant—here, in front of the whole town. I felt humiliated and I disappointed my parents. You're right. I was punishing you for what I couldn't change about myself." I stood up and looked at him, my face wet and feeling weak—too weak to even stand. "You need to go, Colt Stillman. Not because I don't want you here, but because I don't deserve to have you stay." I broke down again and pressed past him to go inside. I ran up the stairs to my own bedroom and threw myself on my bed. I didn't want to hear the sound of his car leaving.

I didn't. What I heard instead was the sound of my bedroom door opening. It was Colt and when I felt his hand on my back, I melted. "I'm so, so sorry," I cried, throwing my arms around his neck and burying my wet cheek against his muscled, male neck. I wanted to stay there, hiding from myself and hiding from the past.

Colt sat still for long moments, but then he couldn't help himself. He opened his frozen arms and wrapped me in them. His face turned, and he kissed my wet cheek, my eyes and my mouth. Colt pushed me back on the bed and held his body over mine, rigid, with one hand on either side of my head. I looked up, questioning.

"I can't leave you, damn it!" he rasped and pulled me against him as he rolled to the bed. "God help me, but I can't walk away."

I molded myself against his hard body, wanting his strength and protection. I was lost, and he was my home.

The cold melted between us and in its place, came the heat. Inch by inch as our clothing was peeled away, came the searing touch of one another's skin. Colt wrapped me inside his flesh and I undulated in the sensation, trying to get as close as possible so we'd never again come apart. There was no time for the gentle teasing, the titillation that precedes the climax. Colt slid into me with a firmness that claimed me—not just my woman's tunnel, but the core of who I was. Over and over he claimed me, each thrust stronger and longer than the previous. This time, when the coming began, it brought with it every nerve in my body, fingertips to toes. I think for a moment I actually did become a part of his body, or he a part of mine. I heard myself cry out at the peak and Colt stiffened as it overcame him as well. We held on as it rocked us, relaxing only as the wave went back out to sea.

Eventually, Colt sank onto his side, pulling me against him and moving my damp hair away from my face. "You didn't keep your promise, you know," he whispered.

I looked up at him, seeing the hurt in his eyes. "Promise?"

"You swore to never run away, to not ever leave me again."

I looked away. "I know, you're right, I didn't."

His big hand pulled my head toward his chest. It was a gesture of forgiveness.

"I'm sorry. It's just that... with everything that's happened, I've been so scared. Carrie and all... I didn't know who to trust. I couldn't trust myself anymore—I'd let myself down more than once. So, I ran and hid, just like a child."

He stroked the back of my head.

"Colt?"

"I'm right here."

"I think I know what's going on. Or rather, who's behind all that went on. I don't know why it didn't occur to me earlier, but I didn't know he was around."

"Who?"

"His name is Paul."

"Carrie's father," he said quietly.

"You knew?"

I felt him nod. "I knew. What makes you think it was him?"

"Just a while ago, Patsy and I were talking, and I found out he's not in the Army anymore. I think he's been doing the stuff that scared me. I don't know about the apartment, but the newspaper envelope, the phone calls, heck, I don't know what all. He was a little strange in the head, Colt. I didn't see it until it was too late. It might have been the reason they let him out of the Army. He targets me, not Carrie. I think he's been watching me."

Colt stiffened at the same moment the words left my mouth. He pushed me away and rolled over me to his feet. I looked at him in amazement. He turned and said one word that drove a torch of terror through me that was so blinding, I thought I would die. "Carrie!"

Colt was already out of the bedroom, pounding down the stairs. "The park!" he shouted back at me. "Where is it?"

I was already pulling on my clothes, running after him down the stairs. "I'm coming with you."

We made it as far as the front door when it opened and there stood Patsy with Carrie. She took one look at our disarray and asked, "Should I come back?"

"No!" Colt barked, pulling the two of them into the house and shutting the door. He took Carrie and handed her to me but faced Patsy. "Did you see Paul, Carrie's father, while you were out?"

Patsy's face filled with alarm at his tone. "It's okay, Patsy, tell him everything," I urged her.

She nodded. "Well, yes. I did. He was sitting in his car at the end of the block, watching Carrie and me. We were across the street from him. I was pushing her in the stroller to the park."

"Oh, my God," came from my mouth.

Colt whipped around. "No. You will not be scared anymore. Not as long as I'm here. Go upstairs and pack your things and Carrie's. You're going home with me."

I took one look at his face and nodded, handing Carrie back to Patsy and turning to run up the staircase as fast as I could.

I heard them talking as I scurried from closet to closet. Colt asked, "Patsy, I'm sorry, but can you go home? If not, you can come with us, but I can't leave these two alone anymore. I think he's behind this and they're not safe—well, at least not Gwen."

"No, no, I can go home right now," Patsy answered. "Take care of them. Let me just get my things."

Chapter 27

Coulter

I watched her walk down the aisle between the rows of white chairs toward me. I was holding my breath, afraid she'd have a last-minute change of heart and bolt off into the woods.

She didn't. She continued toward me, taking the wedding march strides with her long, stunning legs. I had to look away to control myself from growing erect in front of the entire assemblage.

I held out my hand to her and as Carrie, in her tiny white patent leather shoes threw another clump of rose petals onto the ground, Gwen's stunning eyes looked into mine. I saw love, I saw need, I saw—best of all, trust. A few words later and we were man and wife. I kissed her in front of the world and it felt like a chain that would bind us the way we were meant to be from the beginning.

As the guests applauded, I bent to pick up Carrie and held her as I put my arm around Gwen. Facing everyone I spoke out loudly. "Thank you all for being here today to share this with us. Today I have the wife I've always wanted, and I hope to share my name with Carrie as well."

The applause doubled, then faded suddenly as a figure

emerged from the stand of trees at the edge of the seating. "I might just have something to say about that," called out a man with a rough beard, a bottle of liquor in his hand and a holstered gun evident across his chest.

I heard Gwen gasp. "Paul!"

"Having a little trouble there, Gwen? Wonder why you never heard my voice at the other end of those phone calls? Did you think pretty boy there dirtied your pretties in that shabby apartment? Did he save all the newspapers—the clippings of you in your cheerleading get-up, flipping around on the football field? Well?"

I said in a low, but very distinct voice, "Gwen, take Carrie and stand behind me. He won't fire if he thinks he'd hit her." I motioned to Buddy who was my best man. "Get her out of here, now!"

I stood my ground, center stage as Buddy flagged a few men and suddenly Gwen and Carrie were herded into their protective circle and moved backward, into the house.

"You want me, Romano? Come get me," I challenged him, walking down the wedding aisle toward him.

"You? Hell, no! I don't want you! I want her!" Romano pulled the gun and fired it into the air, waving the bottle with his left hand. I took advantage of the moment and charged him, knocking him to the ground and batting away the gun. It was only moments before my men were on us, pulling me off. I wanted to kill him there, while God was still watching.

"Get him off the property!" I ordered. "Keep the gun."

Paul was dragged to the road and when they let go of his arms, he brushed himself off in disgust and disappeared briefly into the pines, emerging aboard a motorcycle. He spun out as powered it off the estate, nearly flipping it.

I brushed myself off, apologized to our guests and signaled the small orchestra nearby to begin playing. Waiters appeared with trays of champagne flutes and I headed up the middle to get my bride—my family.

Chapter 28

Gwen

It all happened in slow motion, or at least that's how it appeared to me. I peeked through the sheers over the window and watched as Colt wrestled Paul to the ground, and then shortly thereafter, Paul sped off on his motorcycle.

Then my husband came for me. He lifted me off my feet and kissed me. A cheer went up around us from the men who'd been protecting Carrie and me. Colt, with me still in his arms, walked out onto the porch and a second cheer went up. He turned and as tradition dictated, carried me over the threshold.

Finally, it was as it should be. Finally, I could rest.

The reception roared into reality and people forgot the unpleasantness from earlier. Banquet tables, laden with the finest foods were gathering spots as people milled around, talking and laughing. Colt had buses lined up to drive everyone home later, so drinking was the sport of the afternoon. I changed my clothes and Colt and I danced and celebrated with the entire town. Patsy had Carrie by the hand as they wandered the grounds, amidst peacocks, fountains, and clusters of white chairs where the celebrants feasted and drank.

Despite the shaking that still coursed through me, I leaned into my husband and knew unjudging love.

Then came the sheriff's car, through the gates and slowly in our direction. He climbed out and came toward us. Colt gave me a quick hug of reassurance and turned to face the sheriff.

"You look like you're here on business," Colt greeted him.

"'Fraid so. I believe you had an incident here earlier this afternoon."

Colt nodded. "You could call it that. What's wrong, Sheriff?"

"We just peeled Paul Romano off a tree about a mile east of here. Found his bike a good hundred yards further down, in the brush. You know anything about this?"

Colt froze. He slowly turned to me and there was doubt in his brilliant blue eyes as he searched my face.

I threw my arms around his neck, kissed him on the cheek and then stood at his side, taking his hand in mine. "You've got yourself the wrong people, Sheriff. No one here has left and no one here would go after Paul Romano. He's not worth it."

Colt squeezed my hand and the sheriff nodded. “Didn’t think so,” he said. “Congratulations to you two,” he added and walked back to his car.

“Gwennie?” whispered Colt in my ear.

“Yes?”

“I love you.”

“I love you, too, Mr. Stillman.”

Epilogue

"Now Gwen, I don't want you to push this time, you hear me?"

"What do you mean?" I gasped. "You've been telling me to push for the last half hour. You'd better get ready to catch!"

Dr. Welter looked up over my stirrup-locked legs at Colt and grinned. "Does she always argue like this?"

"She sure does," I heard Colt respond just as the next wave of pain rolled through my body.

Two minutes later, Colt was holding his son. "He's a Stillman, alright," he judged, looking at the baby's squirming body and then at me. "Want to know how I can tell?"

That's when Coulter Stillman, Jr. let out a loud, shrill bellow. With triumphant sweat rolling off my face I answered, "He's also got your bossiness?"

THE END

89015682R00136

Made in the USA
Lexington, KY
21 May 2018